SPOOKED

The Haunting of Kit Connelly

Also by Paul Bryers

THE MYSTERIES OF THE SEPTAGRAM TRILOGY
Kobal
Avatar
Abyss

SPOOKED

The Haunting of Kit Connelly

PAUL BRYERS

Hodder
Children's
Books

A division of Hachette Children's Books

For Lauren

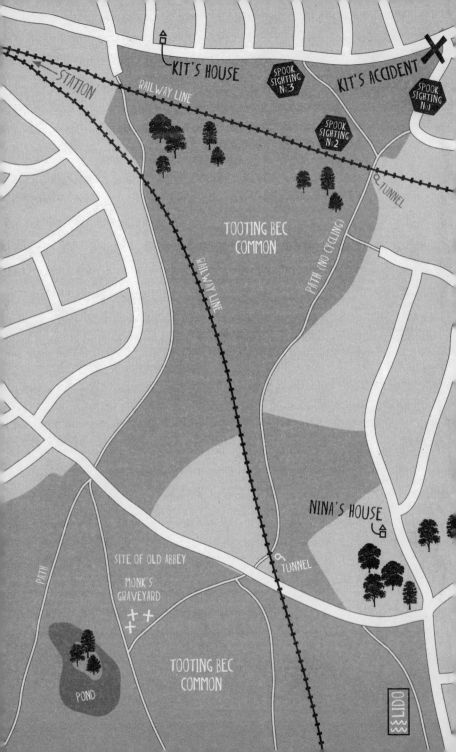

1

The Wheels on the Bus

They say that when you've only got seconds to live your whole life flashes before you. I don't know about that. All I could remember was a sense of not being there. Of being somewhere else. The strange thing was – it was the last place I wanted to be. Well, not the last place, obviously. The last place I wanted to be was where I was – lying in the middle of a road with my foot trapped in the front wheel of a bike and a large double-decker bus hurtling towards me. But one part of my mind was in the other place. Pre-school playgroup. I could even hear the words of the song we used to sing before the mid-morning break.

The wheels on the bus go round and round
Round and round, round and round

Miss McIntyre used to make us sing it before she handed out the orange juice and biscuits.

The horn on the bus goes beep, beep, beep
Beep beep beep, beep beep beep

And we'd have to mime the actions that went with the words.

I used to hate it. Sapphire Enron and Amy Dyer in their Gap jeans and T-shirts and their cute little high heels hopping about like they were in an all-girl band and Kieran Connor who's always one step behind going *beep, beep, beep* for the horn while everyone else was going *glug, glug, glug* for the petrol pump.

Everyone except me, that is.

I used to keep my lips pressed firmly shut and my arms tightly folded all the way through. And when it was finished Miss McIntyre used to say in her sweet little voice: '*Very good girls and boys, very, very good. That was even better than yesterday. But one of us wasn't singing, was she, Catherine? One of us wasn't joining in like the rest of us and Having Fun.*'

As if it was Fun singing those stupid words and putting your arms in front of you and going *swish, swish, swish* like the windscreen wipers, or covering your eyes with your hands when the doors shut and uncovering them when they open.

My friend Nina, who's known me since I was born, practically, says I was always a facety kid, even at four and a half.

But honestly, you'd think, wouldn't you, if you'd only got seconds to live, that you'd be spared the thought of Miss McIntyre and Sapphire Enron and Kieran Connor and the rest of the numpties going *swish, swish, swish.* The last thought in your head before you go *swish, swish, splat!* and they sweep you up and cart you off to the morgue. And Miss McIntyre peering down at you with that sad, sorrowful look in her baby blue eyes:

'You see what happens, Catherine? You see what happens when you don't sing "The Wheels on the Bus"?'

Then she's telling me to get up and screaming at me like she's finally flipped, calling me a stupid cow and a freak and other names you only ever get in the playground when the teachers aren't within hearing distance.

It was this that made me realize, of course, that it wasn't Miss McIntyre at all. This and the fact that she was about fifty years younger and wearing black lipstick with the thickest make-up you've ever seen and choppy blonde hair with a red streak. Oh, and a ring through her nose.

And then, as I'm staring up at her, I see that she's got three more rings in one of her ears and another through her right eyebrow. She's wearing a black leather skirt with an off-the-shoulder top, spider's-web tights and big black leather buckle boots with skulls on them.

And on her left shoulder is a large tattoo of a death's-head moth.

Even if you met her in Hell, Miss McIntyre was never going to look like that, not in a million years.

She's still ranting away at me and I'm staring up at her, speechless, cos I actually did think I was in Hell for a minute, even if I don't believe in it. I thought I'd died and gone to Hell and she was one of the demons.

Then somehow – more from sheer terror of the demon, I think, than fear of being crushed under the wheels of a bus – I've got my foot free of the spokes and I'm rolling out of the way a fraction of a second before the bus skids to a halt at the exact place I'd just been lying.

Then it gets *very* confusing. The bus has stopped and there's a crowd of people asking me if I'm all right. And I'm saying Sorry and Thank you, like that's all the words I was ever taught. I meant them for the girl, really, but then I realized she wasn't there. At least I couldn't see her, and she wasn't the kind of person it was easy to miss.

'What in God's name were you thinking about?'

This is the bus driver. He's jumped down from the cab and he's glaring at me with his fists clenched like he wants to finish the job.

'Didn't you see me?'

'Yes – but . . .'

'She just turned right in front of me,' he says to the crowd. 'And the next thing she's lying in the middle of the road.'

'It was that thing there,' I said.

They all looked. It was one of those metal things they put in the middle of the road especially for cyclists to skid on – manhole covers, I think they're called. (I don't know why – like there's a man living down there? I don't think so.) It was all wet with rain. I don't think I mentioned that it was raining. A thin drizzle that you'd hardly know was there until you realized how wet you were.

'It was like ice,' I said.

Then they all turn on me. Now they know I'm all right, they're on the bus driver's side.

'Poor man – he could have killed you.'

'You should have waited till it was safe to cross.'

'Didn't you see it coming?'

'Does your mammy know you're riding your bike on the main road?'

For heaven's sake, I'm nearly twelve, not three!

But they had a point. I'm not supposed to use the main road when I go to Nina's. I'm supposed to cut across the Common. But there's a ban on riding bikes in the Common, except in certain areas, and the other day I got stopped by the parks police.

'What does that say?' they said, pointing at the sign on the track I was riding down. It said, No Cycling. But it was upside down from where I was standing.

'Gnilcyc On,' I said, pretending to read it upside down.

I thought that was quite good on the spur of the moment.

But they didn't, of course. They're parks police.

'I see,' says one. 'A clever clogs.'

'Name and address,' says the first, taking out his notebook.

I had it off pat. 'Sapphire Enron, seventy-eight Wickham Road, Balham.'

'And if we catch you again, you're in real trouble,'

they said. Which was probably right, because if they did catch me again they were bound to make me take them back to seventy-eight Wickham Road, Balham, and then they'd find out the last number in the street is seventy-six.

'Next time you stick to the Designated Cycle Lanes,' they said.

Which would be fine if the Designated Cycle Lanes went anywhere near where I wanted to go.

So next time I went round by the main road and look what happened. They'd rather have kids spattered under the wheels of a bus than let them ride across the Common in the No Cycling lane.

'You'll cop it from your dad when he sees that bike.'

This is the bus driver. I looked at it. The front wheel was all buckled where the bus had gone over it. I thought what it would have done to my head.

'Think how he'd feel if you were dead,' says one of the others – the Bus Driver's Support Club. 'Think how your poor mammy would feel.'

'Never mind her poor mammy, think how *I'd* feel,' says the bus driver.

'Sorry,' I said again. But rolling my eyes a bit, because I'd had enough by now. And off I go, pushing my bike along the pavement, and the bus drives off with all the passengers staring out of the window at me and the bus driver shaking his fist.

I felt a bit sick then. With shock I suppose. I kept thinking about lying in the road and seeing that bus coming at me. I had to take deep breaths. And the really annoying thing was I still had the words of that song going through my head, I just couldn't get rid of them.

The wheels on the bus go round and round . . .

And that girl. I suppose she'd saved my life. No doubt about it. The front wheel of the bus ended up exactly where my head was about a second earlier. No wonder she was swearing at me. But she'd said something else, too; what was it? Something about having a death-wish. More than that. I couldn't quite remember it now. Something really personal – *as if she knew me*. But I was pretty sure I'd never seen her before. You'd surely remember if you had.

And how come she'd suddenly vanished when all the others gathered round?

After a while I felt a bit better. The rain had stopped and the sun had come out and there was a rainbow in the sky and the birds were singing. It felt good to be alive. And yet, in a strange kind of way, I didn't feel like I *was* alive. It felt more like being in a dream. As if nothing was real.

I think it was then that I first thought I might be dead.

2

Goths, Emos and Wailing Monks

'What have you done to your bike?'

This is Nina when I get to her house.

'I ran into a bus,' I said.

'You liar.' Looking at me to see if I am. Lying, I mean. Then she looks at the bike again. 'The front wheel's all buckled,' she says.

'You should see the bus,' I said. I was feeling a bit better now.

She just gave me a look and I stuck the bike out of the way at the back of the hall.

'Well, are you going to tell me what happened or aren't you?' she says.

But I could hear Nina's mum, Shella, in the kitchen

and I didn't want her to hear. She's great, Shella, but she's part of the mums' network. She's a teacher, too. She teaches part time at a school for kids with special needs. I didn't want Shella knowing I'd fallen under a bus. She'd be on to my mum in no time.

'Upstairs,' I said.

So we go up to her bedroom. I love Nina's bedroom. It's a sort of secret place, or a place for telling secrets, anyway. It used to be yellow but we did a makeover in the summer and now it's all red. Red walls, red ceiling and this fantastic rug on the floor that's made of silk and one of her uncles brought back from a village in Pakistan, near the Chinese border. That's what Nina says anyway. It probably came from John Lewis, she's such a liar. And there's this great duvet cover with a peacock on it, but we sit on these cushions on the floor cos she doesn't like her bed messed up.

'So go on,' she says, as she closes her bedroom door. 'This bus.'

So I told her about it. And the girl who saved my life.

'The bus stopped just where my head was a second before,' I said. 'It would have gone splat like a melon.'

'More like a coconut,' said Nina thoughtfully. She likes to get things right.

But I could see she thought I was exaggerating so I pulled up my jeans and started peering at my knee to see if there was a bruise coming up.

'But didn't you see it coming?' she said, just like one of the women from Rent-a-Crowd, only with this eagle-eyed lawyer's stare. Her dad says she'd make a brilliant lawyer cos she's always arguing with him and picking him up on things, but she wants to be a set designer for the movies. She reckons she has a flair for it. But I reckon her dad's right: she should be a lawyer.

'Yes, but I thought I could make it,' I said and I told her about the manhole cover and the rain.

'So the bike's on top of you,' she says slowly. 'And you've got your foot caught in the wheel, and the bus is coming straight at you?'

Like I'm in the witness box and she's taking me through the story bit by bit so she can take it apart.

'And this girl just appears from nowhere and pulls you clear?'

'That's right. Well, she didn't exactly pull me; she just kind of yelled at me to get up.'

(What she actually yelled was, 'Move your arse' –

or at least that was some of what she yelled at me. Even Nina would be shocked at the rest.)

'You needed yelling at, did you?' said Nina. 'You were happy just lying there?'

'Well, I was a bit stunned.'

'So what was she like, this girl? Well built, was she? Looked like she works out? Pumps a lot of iron?'

I knew she was being sarcastic and she still didn't believe me. That's the thing about being a liar – you think everybody else is, too. 'No. Not really,' I said, all cool. I described her, right down to the ring in her nose and the death's-head moth tattoo.

'Sounds like she's a goth,' says Nina.

'More like an emo,' I said.

There's not a lot of difference to look at, but you know it when you see it. And emos are more aggressive. At least in my opinion. I know they have this reputation for being all emotional and sensitive and wanting to kill themselves but in my opinion it's you they want to kill.'

'Was she on the bus?' says Nina.

I looked at her. 'No. Of course she wasn't on the bus. How could she have been on the bus when she was standing next to me?'

'I don't know.' She shrugged. 'She might have seen you fall and jumped off to save you. Like a superhero.'

'Yeah. Right.'

'So she was just passing by?'

'I suppose. Or maybe she's my guardian angel and she swooped down from the sky.'

I can be just as sarcastic as Nina if I put my mind to it.

'Looking like an emo?'

Now I'm doing the shrug but to tell the truth I was beginning to have my doubts. That's what lawyers do: they put doubts in your mind and feed them. Maybe it was the knock on the head.

'I'm not imagining her, you know,' I snapped at her.

'I didn't say you were.'

There was an awkward silence. Then she said: 'And then she just kind of . . . vanished?'

'Well, I wouldn't say vanished, exactly. I just couldn't see her. There was a crowd of people all round me.'

Nina sniffed. 'You should tweet it,' she said. 'Like people do with missing cats. Or hamsters.'

She never misses a trick, Nina. This is because the

last time my hamster went missing I posted it on Twitter. I thought it might be living wild on the Common.

And yes, I know hamsters don't read tweets, but my friends do and I thought one of them might have seen it.

Nina's still going on. 'Anyone seen "escaped emo in Tooting with ring through nose and death's-head moth tattoo?" How many characters is that? If she lives locally people must have seen her about.' Then she shook her head. 'But I can't see her coming from round here. Streatham maybe, or the outer fringes of suburbia.'

The outer fringes of suburbia. This is the way she talks. I shrugged again.

'Maybe she doesn't dress like that all the time,' I said. 'Maybe she was on her way somewhere.'

'Like an emo convention, you mean? In Tooting?'

'No. Like someone's party or something.' It was Saturday afternoon; it was possible. 'Anyway, I think I might have seen her around, now I come to think of it.' I screwed my face up. 'Not looking like that exactly, but . . .'

'Where?'

'I don't know where. Just around.'

15

I wasn't lying. I did think I'd seen her around. There was something about her that seemed kind of familiar to me, but it wasn't something I could pin down. And then there were the things she'd said to me – they were starting to come back to me now.

'*Have you got some kind of death wish or what?*'

'*You're going to die soon enough – no need to rush it.*'

Except that she didn't say it as politely as that.

And I couldn't get it out of my head that she knew me.

I was still thinking about this when there's a knock on the door and even though Nina says, 'Go away,' like she always does, it opens and her brother's standing there. Omar. I'm not into boys as a rule but you could make an exception for Omar. He's fifteen and he's gorgeous. Trouble is, he knows it.

'Hello, girls,' he says, leaning on the door with this lazy grin and his eyes all narrow and cool.

Nina gives him the finger but he just grins some more and he looks at me and he says, 'Hi, Kit, how's it going?'

'OK,' I mutter, feeling a blush spreading up from my neck. I hate myself sometimes. Well, most of the time, actually.

'Is that your bike downstairs?'

'Well, whose else would it be, duh?' This from Nina. Her name means Gracious One in Urdu; did I mention that?

'I'm sorry, is it in the way?' I said. 'I'll come down and move it, if you like.'

'No, that's all right, but what did you do to the front wheel?'

'She ran into a bus,' said Nina, smirking.

'Really?' Slight raise of the brows. He's got eyebrows like a girl. Eyelashes too. Which does him no harm at all, in my opinion.

'I hit a bump,' I said, frowning at Nina.

'Some bump,' he said. 'We've got a few spares in the shed. Do you want me to see if I can get one to fit?'

'Could you?' I said sweetly. I ignore the way Nina's rolling her eyes.

A few minutes later I see him out in the back garden taking the wheel off. He worked in a bike shop over the summer so he more or less knows what he's doing, or at least he pretends he does.

'The boy wonder,' says Nina, but a few minutes later she makes an excuse to go downstairs and I see her talking to him in the back garden. I wondered if she was telling him more about the bus. Then she came back upstairs and made me play 'Stardoll' with her on her laptop until I lost the will to live and we played 'Twilight Princess' instead until it was time for me to go home.

When we went downstairs the bike was back in the hall with a new front wheel on it.

'It should be all right,' said Omar when I thanked him. 'But I'll run back with you, if you like, just to make sure.'

I started to say I'd be OK, but he's saying no problemo, he was going for a run anyway, and I could pace him on the bike. Nina snorted but we both ignored her.

'I don't suppose I'll be able to go fast enough,' I said.

'Don't worry,' says Nina, 'he's just got over a groin strain, haven't you, bro?' And she gives him a wicked grin.

I could feel myself going red again but I pretended to be looking over my bike and testing the brakes. I haven't got any brothers myself. I'm not sure if that's a good or a bad thing, but it certainly makes you more relaxed around boys if you have. I was already feeling nervous about the ride across the Common.

We all call it the Common but its real name is the Bec. Tooting Bec. It was named after some monks from a place called Bec in Normandy who came over with William the Conqueror in 1066 and built an abbey here. Nina's mum told me that. She knows more about English history than anyone else I know, even though she was born in Pakistan.

There's no sign of the abbey now, not even a pile of ruins, but there's supposed to be the ghost of a monk who wanders along the side of the lake moaning and wailing. He's called the Wailing Monk of Bec. Or just the Black Monk, cos he wears a black robe and a hood. Lots of people say they've seen him, but quite honestly half the people you see on the Common look like that when they're wearing hoodies so it could be anyone. But Shella says the lake is on the site of an old graveyard where all the monks were buried and he's wandering around looking for his grave. I think she might have made that up, though. She knows I like ghost stories.

So we're heading out across the Common – in the Designated Cycling Lane so the parks police can't have me put away for life. Me cycling and Omar running. The sun's very low in the sky, and the leaves are turning. It's a lovely evening. Everything's wonderful. And then I think maybe I should say something.

That's typical of me. Long silences make me feel embarrassed and I always have to start a conversation. And I nearly always say the wrong thing.

Here are some of the things I could have said:

Wheel seems to be OK.

Isn't the sky lovely?

What a great sunset . . .

Or even:

What's the difference between an emo and a goth?

But I didn't say any of these things. What I said was:

'How's the groin strain?'

I mean, *what??????*

It wasn't as if I'd been thinking about it; it just came out. Like projectile vomit. *'How's the groin strain?'*

'It's OK,' he says. 'Thanks for asking.'

Then I see the girl again. She's standing by herself, just to one side of the path, next to a tree, smoking a cigarette and looking at me through narrowed eyes. She's some distance away and there's no way she could have heard me, but I'm not kidding, she just stares at me like I'm some kind of freak and then she turns round and deliberately bangs her head three times against the trunk of the tree.

3

Screams in the Night

OK, I know I should have gone over and talked to her. Introduced myself. Thanked her for saving my life. Even if she just slagged me off again. But it was a bit difficult with Omar there. He was bound to ask me who she was and how I knew her, and then I'd have either had to lie to him or tell him about the bus.

Besides, it crossed my mind, even then, that she wasn't really there. Not a ghost as such, like the Wailing Monk, but some kind of fantasy I was having. Like a hallucination from the knock on the head. I wondered if I should have gone to hospital to have it checked. Nina obviously thought the girl was all in my mind. I could just imagine the conversation when

Omar got back from seeing me home.

'Did she seem all right to you? I mean, she didn't do anything strange on the way home?'

'No. Apart from when she stopped to talk to a tree.'

So I just put my head down and kept on going and never looked back. I was afraid that if I did she'd have vanished, just like before.

As soon as you come out of the tunnel under the railway line you can see our house. If you know what you're looking for, that is, cos it's one of about fifty houses that run along that side of the Common. You have to cross the road to get to them, but it's only a small road; you don't get any buses on it and there are speed bumps to slow the traffic down. Even so, Omar saw me across like I was about four years old, making me get off my bike and look both ways. I was worried for a minute he was going to hold my hand. He let me go up the front path by myself but when I looked back at the door he was still standing there watching me with a strange look on his face. But then he just grinned and gave me a wave and ran off.

I opened the front door and went in.

'Is that you, Kit?'

This is my mother. Shouting down from upstairs.

'Yes,' I said.

'I hope you're not wheeling that bike through my nice, clean house dropping mud everywhere.'

No, I'm not. I'm *riding* it through the house. I'm riding in circles round the kitchen. I'm riding up the walls. Look at all the wheel marks. Wheeeee.

I carried my bike through the house and out into the garden and stashed it in the bike shed, like I'm supposed to. When I go back in she's coming down the stairs carrying a tray with three cups on it.

'I found these in your room,' she says. 'Three cups hiding under the bed. One of them's got something growing in it.'

'It's probably fungus,' I said. 'You shouldn't have moved it. It's a project I'm doing for homework.'

She gives me a look.

'It's disgusting,' she said.

'Well, don't go in there,' I said, 'if you find it so disgusting.'

I hate her going into my room when I'm not there. I don't go into her room looking to see if there's cups under *her* bed. She's still glaring at me.

'I don't know what you do to get it in such a mess,' she said. 'And look at you. What have you been doing with yourself?'

'What do you mean?' I said.

'Look at your hair. And what's that on your anorak, mud or chocolate?'

I scratched at it with a fingernail and then put my finger in my mouth and pretended to think about it.

'Dog do,' I said.

'Don't be gross. Did you have anything to eat at Nina's?' She looks vaguely around the kitchen as if she's just seeing it for the first time. I know what this means. It means she's not done any shopping and there's nothing for us to eat.

'I had a cold chapatti,' I said.

She opens the fridge door and peers at the empty shelves. 'We've got eggs,' she says a bit doubtfully. 'I could do us an omelette.'

'Great,' I say. There's nothing like an omelette when you've nearly been run over by a bus, especially a plain omelette; it really cheers you up. I thought of telling her this, but it wouldn't sound the same without the bit about the bus and I wasn't going to tell her that, for sure.

'Or we could get in a pizza.'

This is more like it.

She looks at me. 'But you need to shower first.'

'What – to eat a pizza?'

'I'm not eating a pizza with you looking like that.'

Sometimes I wonder about my mother. She's got this thing about keeping everything clean and tidy. Nina calls it OCD, which stands for Obsessive Compulsive Disorder. She doesn't say my mum's got it – she's too polite for that, at least about my mum – but she tells me about other people who have it so I'll know what she means. Anyway, I think she's right about my mum. She never stops wiping things down, or straightening things, or picking them up as soon as you put them down and putting them away somewhere where you can never find them. She says it's because she works at home and if you work at home all day you can't stand to see dirty dishes lying around and all that.

My dad says to me, 'Don't stay in one place too long or she'll wipe you down with a cloth.' It's all right for him; he's never here. He's a photographer – or I should say a photojournalist, cos he mainly photographs things that are in the news, so he's away a lot. I wish I could say this is what makes Mum sad but she seems even sadder when he's at home.

I don't know what's wrong with them, but something is. They don't argue all the time, or scream at each other, like some parents. If anything, they're far too polite. Not like Nina's mum and dad who are either laughing and hugging or shouting at each other and throwing things. That never happens in our house. Not with my mum and dad. It's like something's broken down and they don't know how to fix it.

They're both all right with me, though. Apart from Mum's thing about being tidy. I suppose I've got nothing to complain about really.

'What kind of pizza would you like?' she says.

I went for pizza capricciosa which is mozzarella, tomato, mushrooms, artichokes, ham and olives. Mum ordered a margherita without the cheese. Can you believe that? Pizza margherita without the cheese is basically tomato paste on a crust. And she'll leave most of the crust.

She's been on a diet. She says she wants to get her figure back. If you ask me, if she wants her figure back she should eat ten pork pies a day, cos she hasn't *got* a figure. She just goes straight up and down. Maybe a slight bump here and there. I know Dad would rather she was a bit fatter cos he looks kind of stunned when he sees her nibbling on a lettuce leaf or something. And sometimes when he's staring into the fridge and saying, 'What are we having for dinner?' she says, 'But we had lunch.'

'You don't eat enough to stay alive,' he says.

He eats all the time. All the time he's with us anyway. He's always got his nose in the fridge. But he's thin, too. Not as thin as Mum and much more muscly, but he doesn't seem to put on any weight, no matter how much he eats. He says it's because he's on the go all the time. I think it's because he's always having to dodge bullets. I worry about him. He's been in Libya and Syria. But now he's in Russia so with luck nobody will be shooting at him.

I take more after my dad than my mum. Everyone says so. In appearance and everything. Only not so wiry. I've got the same reddish blonde hair as Dad. And freckles. Not many, but enough to worry about. And I like doing things that are adventurous, like rock climbing and shooting rapids. Not that I've done any real rock climbing, but I've joined the climbing club at school and I do the wall at the gym and they're going to take us to the Lake District to climb real rocks next summer.

I've only done rapids once – that was with my dad in France – but I loved it. He says he'll take me again next summer. Also I play football. Attacking midfield. And of course, cycling. If my dad's not away on a job, we're going on the London-to-Brighton cycle ride this year. That's over fifty miles.

But sometimes I like hanging out with my mum, eating pizza.

I might have given the wrong impression of my mother. She can be quite nice sometimes. She just isn't very happy. Things didn't really work out for her the way she wanted them to.

She used to be a swimmer. I mean a proper swimmer; she swam for England. This was before I was born. She was in line for the Olympics but then she had an accident. She doesn't talk about it much, but it was something to do with her back and she was laid up for months. Then she had me and that put an end to it for good. She doesn't say that, but I'm sure she thinks it.

So now she sells advertising space to sports magazines. She does it on the phone, mostly. That's why she works from home. She's supposed to be good at it and she seems to make enough money. But she doesn't like it. She says it's not exactly *fulfilling* selling advertising space. It's usually for trainers and sports gear – and swimsuits. I suppose that could be quite depressing after you've swum for England. But I don't think that's the real reason she's not happy.

Anyway, she seemed to be a bit more cheerful tonight. I started to lay the table and she said, 'Let's have it in the other room and watch a movie.'

I was amazed. 'What about the crumbs?' I said.

'Don't worry about that,' she said. 'I'll get the Dyson out as soon as it's over.'

So we sat in front of the television eating pizza and watching a movie.

It was called 'Sleeping with the Enemy'. It was a fifteen, but either my mother hadn't noticed or she didn't care. I thought there might be sex in it, which made me a bit tense with my mother sat next to me. But there wasn't. Not much, anyway. It's about this woman whose husband is a psycho. Or a control freak, which is the same thing really. She's so scared of him she daren't ask for a divorce and she can't run away cos she knows he'll find her, so she fakes her own death. They go out in this boat in a storm and she falls overboard and he thinks she's been drowned, but she's clinging to this buoy.

Mum put it on pause then and I thought she'd decided it wasn't suitable for me, which she does sometimes, but no, she's just decided she can't stand to sit there with the dirty pizza plates on the table, so I have to clear them away while she wipes a cloth over the surface, so she can relax and watch the rest of the film.

The man thinks his wife has drowned, even though they never find the body. But in fact she's living in a different town hundreds of miles away under a different name. But then her husband finds out and comes after her. I won't tell you the ending so as not to spoil it for you but it's so scary I nearly wet myself. I think mum was more scared than I was. We were clinging to each other at one point, and she's turning her head away and going, 'Tell me when I can look!' The woman's played by Julia Roberts, who looks a bit like my mum. Or I should say my mum looks a bit like Julia Roberts. She's got the same kind of hair anyway, and the same wide mouth.

We sat there for a while when the film ended, thinking about it.

I was thinking I wouldn't mind if *I* looked a bit like Julia Roberts. Twenty years ago, anyway. Instead of looking like my dad.

'That was scary,' Mum said. 'I should never have let you watch it.'

This is typical of her.

'You'll have nightmares,' she said. 'You'll wake up screaming.'

As if.

'It's all right,' I said. 'It was great.'

'Up you go, then,' she said. 'I'll be up in a minute to kiss you goodnight.'

As I was on my way upstairs I heard the vacuum cleaner going. She must have seen a crumb on the floor.

Before I went to bed I pulled back the curtain a little and looked out of the window, cos I had this crazy idea the girl was standing outside, watching the house. My bedroom is at the front of the house and I could see this long line of streetlights going out across the Common. There was a thin rain in the air, like a mist. I looked out for quite some time, until I heard my mum coming up the stairs to kiss me goodnight, but I couldn't see anyone. It must have been the film, making me nervous.

When I was lying in bed, though, I couldn't help thinking about her. Imagining her out there in the rain and the darkness in the middle of the empty Common. Her and the Wailing Monk.

And then, just as I was nodding off, I heard this terrible screaming.

I was wide awake in a flash. I knew I wasn't dreaming. It was coming from outside. I jumped out of bed and scuttled over to the window and pressed my face to the glass so I could look out.

The rain was heavier now and I couldn't see much at first, just the streetlights, all bleary and faded, and the shiny surface of the road and the darkness over the Common. Then I saw this fox. It was walking straight down the middle of the road and screaming. I remembered now that I'd heard something like it once before and Mum had said it was a vixen – a she-fox – and that they did sometimes scream like that, to attract the males. It wouldn't attract me if I was a male fox. I'd be off down the nearest foxhole.

Then I saw the girl.

She was standing under one of the streetlights on the side nearest the Common, just standing there in the rain and looking towards our house.

I couldn't tell for sure – I mean, I couldn't see her face, not at that distance in the dark and the rain – but I knew it was her.

I let the curtain fall back so she wouldn't see me looking.

But the last thing I saw was the fox walking right past her, as if she wasn't there.

4

Committed to Excellence

'Seen your guardian angel lately?' says Nina when
we're let out for the mid-morning break.

'Pardon?' I said.

When I say 'Pardon?' in a certain tone of
voice instead of 'What?' it's not being polite, it's
a warning. It means you're in serious danger of
annoying me. The next step is 'Excuse me?' After
that anything can happen.

But Nina's not big on warnings.

'Your guardian angel,' she said. 'Your goth or your
emo or whatever she is. Wonder Woman. Super-
heroine. The Girl with the Death's-Head Tattoo.'

'It was a death's-head moth,' I said. 'No. I haven't.
Not since the bus.'

I thought I'd better not mention the other times.

'Maybe she's out there,' said Nina.

'Out there' was the school playground. One of them, anyway; I think there're about six altogether. We're standing on the edge of it, as close to the buildings as we can get, like a couple of nerds at the edge of the swimming pool, afraid someone's going to push us in. Nina's got her arms wrapped round her and she's shivering. I'm trying to look hard.

Nina and I have been going to the same school since Year One. Even before that, if you count Miss McIntyre's pre-school playgroup. We always looked out for each other at Pinewood, which was the primary we went to, and we never had any bother from anybody, not even the teachers. My dad said we were the Queen Bees, whatever that means. But Waverley was something else. We'd only started a couple of weeks ago, and we were still trying to work it out. They've got all these signs up everywhere saying Committed to Excellence, like it's the school motto, but from where we were standing the school looked like the Lion's Den – and I mean Millwall football ground, not the zoo.

The playground was full of kids. All shapes and

sizes but most of them bigger than us. There must have been about two thousand of them out there. All psychos. I'm probably exaggerating. About the number, not the psychos. I think there's only fifteen–hundred kids in the whole school, but that's over a thousand more than we had at primary.

Some kid kicked a ball at me. Hard. I trapped it neatly, flicked it up and kicked it back. At his head. He swore at me. It reminded me of the Girl.

'How could you tell?' I said. 'They all look like her.'

This was definitely an exaggeration. They're not big on piercings at Waverley. It doesn't fit in with being Committed to Excellence. You can't even wear earrings. You have to take them out before you come to school. The emos stick bright coloured sticking plasters over the holes. But there were lots of kids who *could* have been her. I wouldn't have been surprised if there were a fair number of tattoos hidden under the school uniforms. And they all swore like her.

As usual Nina said exactly what was going on in my head.

'If this is Committed to Excellence,' she said, 'it isn't working.'

There were some teachers on patrol, but they tended to keep well out of the danger zones and just pick on the smaller kids, lurking in the fringes, like us. I could see them heading our way.

'Let's mingle,' I said, moving away from the wall. Nina looked at me like I was mad. But she followed me fast enough when I walked off.

There were some kids from our old school huddled in a group. They'd been kicking a ball around but some bigger kid had stamped on it and it had burst. I'm not surprised – that he'd stamped on it, I mean – it had Man U written on it. Most of the kids round here are Chelsea supporters. It's asking for trouble to bring a Man U ball into a school like this. It was still there, all flattened and deflated and the kids were standing around and staring at it, as if it could have been one of them. I knew how they felt.

'Hi,' says Nina and I nodded. We knew them of course – you knew everyone at our last school – but we'd never had much to do with them. I wasn't going to be best buddies with them now, but I had a notion that it was probably best to stick together – for the first few weeks, anyway, before I could form my own gang. I was hoping to get in the Year Seven football team and then I'd have some proper mates. I'd taken up kick-boxing in the summer holidays but I hadn't quite got the hang of it yet and anyway you're not supposed to kick people when you're not in the ring. They've got a strict rule about it. It doesn't do any harm to let people see you practising though.

But probably not in the Waverley school playground. The one thing I'd learned since we started here was not to bring attention to yourself. Try to blend in. Look down, not up. Never look directly into someone's eyes. Specially not if they're a Year Ten girl. Don't show off. Don't bring a Man U football into school. Not that I would of course.

'Whose was it?' I said.

'Kieran's,' they said.

I might have known. I'd known Kieran almost as long as I'd known Nina. He was the one who went *beep*, *beep*, *beep* during 'The Wheels on the Bus' when everyone else was doing *glug*, *glug*, *glug*. I'd put him down as a Man U supporter even then. I looked at him. He was a big, angry sort of boy. He looked angry now but there was nowhere for him to go with it. Except against us, I thought. I'd have to keep an eye on Kieran. He'd been a bit of a bully at the last school but he'd never bothered me, or anyone close to me. He had that much sense – just.

The thing with bullies is to take them on straight away or they'll keep on at you. It doesn't matter if they're bigger than you and they can hurt you. It's better to take a bit of hurt – or even a lot of hurt – in one go rather than a long drawn-out hurt. What you've got to let them know is that you'll fight back whatever they do to you. Kicking, biting, scratching, everything. If you're a girl, my dad says, you've got to fight dirty. And if you can get in one good punch, or kick, where it really hurts, so much the better.

It doesn't matter if you're crying or even howling with pain, it just adds to the effect, so long as you keep fighting. You have to be like Tabaqui the Jackal in *The Jungle Book*. My dad used to read it to me when I went to bed. Tabaqui's in the first story, when Mowgli comes to live with the wolves. All the other animals are afraid of Tabaqui because he's got this madness in him, and when he goes mad he forgets his own fear and runs through the jungle biting everything that comes in his way. This is what Rudyard Kipling says about Tabaqui:

Even the tiger runs and hides when little Tabaqui goes mad.

Well, that's what I was like in primary school. Little Tabaqui. The one and only time anyone ever tried to bully me I went totally mental, and no one ever tried anything after that. They knew the only way of stopping me was to put me in hospital, and on the whole they don't want to do that, if only because of the trouble they'd be in.

But I wasn't too sure it would work at Waverley. It was obvious at a glance that there were some serious psychos here. They might not mind putting you in hospital; they might even enjoy it. I'd just have to put my trust in the teachers and the No Tolerance Zone, but I wasn't happy about it.

'You going to the trials tomorrow?' said Michelle Franklin.

'Yeah,' I said.

'You know they do separate teams?' she said, scowling.

I did. Separate teams for girls and boys. I thought it was pathetic, but there was nothing you could do about it. The trouble with football at this level is that it favours strength and pace. It's all right for Michelle Franklin; she's bigger and faster than most boys her age – she played lone striker in our last team and most boys, they don't get near her. I'm no pushover and I've got a fair turn of speed with the ball, but I'm not that strong going into the tackle. I'm good at distribution and I can read a game all right, but kids at this level, they don't let you dwell on the ball – they're hurling themselves in at you, never mind the ball – and if you want my opinion, the officials need to come down harder on it. They say, 'It's an integral part of the English game, tackling.' Well, I could tell you what I think of that but it wouldn't make it into print. If you want my opinion, it's to keep girls from competing on equal terms with the boys, cos they know it throws you off your game. I'd lost count of the times I'd been chopped down last season. Slide tackling should be banned, in my opinion.

If I was playing in Spain or Italy it wouldn't matter, cos they're not big on tackles over there; they stay on their feet, they track back, they cut down on your options and wait for you to make a mistake. You want to read Xabi Alonso on tackling and staying on your feet. He's my role model, Xabi Alonso. He's got real class. Omar looks a bit like Xabi Alonso, when he was younger. Some of you won't know who I'm talking about but he played for Bilbao and Liverpool and now he plays for Real Madrid and Spain. He can take punishment, too, and he can dish it out.

But this is the point – and I'm being painfully honest here – a girl my size is at a serious disadvantage when it comes to the physical side of the game. And it's no good going into Tabaqui the Jackal mode, cos you'll only get sent off. Even some lame official's going to cut up rough if you try to bite off someone's ear. You can do it later, of course, when they come out of the dressing room, but it doesn't help when you're out on the pitch.

But don't start me on football.

I was so busy thinking about this I didn't see them coming. The Goon Squad.

'What's the matter with you lot?' A woman teacher – I didn't know her name. She's about five foot tall, but tough as old boots. She's got two male teachers as back-up but she doesn't look like she needs them. She's wearing a black tracksuit and running shoes with a whistle round her neck. 'What are you doing hanging about here? Why aren't you playing something?'

'Someone burst our ball, miss.' This is Kieran's mate, Gareth, who's got even less sense than Kieran.

'Someone burst our ball, miss,' she mimicked him. She looked at it and her lips curled. 'Man U fans, are you?' Like they deserve all they're going to get.

I winced. Michelle Franklin pretended to throw up.

'Well, don't stand there like mourners at a funeral. If you've nothing better to do you can run round the playground five times. Off you go. Come on.' And she starts running backwards and going:

'Pick up your books and follow me;
You're in the Waverley infantry.'

I rolled my eyes at Nina but the back-up team's moving in and snapping at our heels, so it's not as if there's any choice in the matter and next thing we're jogging round the playground going:

'Get those feet up off the ground;
Waverley kids don't fool around.'

It was like 'The Wheels on the Bus' all over again – with attitude. But it felt better than standing round like a crowd of numpties, at least as far as I was concerned. And no chance of getting beaten up by the psychos, not with Waverley's answer to Lori Alan running in front of us giving us the words. Nina was furious though, cos we were all sweaty for the rest of the day. She said we smelt like the changing room at the gym.

She was still moaning on about it on the way home. To Nina's home, that is. The deal is I usually go back to her place so we can do our homework together and Mum picks me up in the car an hour or so later when she's finished for the day. So we're dragging ourselves along the pavement with about two tons of homework on our backs — cos that's another thing about Waverley: they load you down with homework, two hours a night you have to do in the first term — and Nina's still going on about smelling like old socks and I looked up and I saw her. The Girl.

She was standing at the bus stop on the other side of the road. But she looked different. It was weird, now I think about it, that I recognized her at all. In the first place she was wearing a school uniform. A *Waverley* school uniform, just like ours, except the skirt was nothing like as long. But I knew it was the same girl. There was something about her. Maybe it was the shape of her face, or the way she was standing. Or the way she was looking at me. As if I was something nasty she'd nearly stepped in.

I'd stopped dead in the middle of the pavement. Nina was still walking on, banging on about Waverley, and then she realized I wasn't with her any more and she turned round and looked back at me all annoyed, cos she must have realized how mad she looked talking away to herself like that.

'What's the matter with you?' she said. Then she

saw my face. 'You look as if you've seen a . . .'

Then it dawned on her and she whirls round to see what I'm staring at. But just at that moment a bus pulls in at the stop and we can't see her any more.

'Is that the bus?' says Nina. 'The one that nearly—'

'It's her,' I said. 'The Girl.'

Nina looks again, but of course we can't see her because of the bus and when it pulls away she's not there any more.

'What girl?' says Nina, though she knows very well what girl.

'The emo,' I said. 'The Girl with the Moth Tattoo.'

'Oh her,' she says. 'Well, I expect she caught the bus,' she said in this calm, kind voice she uses when she's trying to humour me, cos I've totally lost it.

'Yes, but − she was wearing a school uniform,' I stammered.

'Well, I expect she goes to school,' says Nina, like she's a nurse trying to talk me down from the ceiling. 'How old did you say she was?'

'About fourteen or fifteen,' I said.

'Well, there you are then.'

'But it was *our* school uniform,' I said.

'Well, perhaps she goes to *our* school,' she said. 'Wouldn't that be nice for you?'

I'm going to hit her in a minute. I haven't hit Nina since she was six, even though she's asked for it on a more or less daily basis, but if she goes on like this I'm going to give her something to moan about.

And then I realized what was bothering me, like it had been in the back of my mind ever since I'd first seen her, even with the dyed blonde hair and all the piercings. The feeling that she reminded me of someone I knew.

Because I'd finally realized who it was.

It was me.

5

Happy Families

'What do you mean, she looks like you?' Nina's staring at me as if I've said something really stupid. 'You don't look anything like an emo. No emo would be seen dead looking like you.'

'Thanks,' I said. 'But she didn't look like one either – not this time.'

'Then how do you know it was her?'

'I just know,' I said.

I could see she thought I'd lost it, so I told her about the time I'd seen her on the Common, banging her head against a tree.

'Why was she banging her head against a tree?'

'Don't ask,' I said, cos I wasn't going to tell her I'd asked her brother about his groin strain. Instead

I told her about the next time I'd seen her, standing outside our house late at night. 'She was standing next to a lamppost,' I said, 'and this fox walked straight past her.'

'Well, at least it didn't walk straight through her,' she said. Ha, ha.

'You don't believe me?'

'Sure I believe you.' We walked on in silence for a while. Then she goes: 'But no one else saw her, did they? Not your mum or your dad, or Omar, or anyone on the bus when you first saw her? And *I* didn't see her either, at the bus stop.'

'You would have seen her if a bus hadn't come,' I pointed out. But I could tell she wasn't convinced.

'Well, there are three possibilities,' she says in what her dad calls her courtroom voice, the one she uses to persuade people to see things the way she sees them. 'One, you're having hallucinations; two, she's your big sister no one's ever told you about; and three – she's a ghost.'

'What?' I meant this to cover them all really, but she took it to mean the last one.

'A ghost,' she said. 'A phantom. A *spook*.'

And she waves her arms about and makes ghost noises – 'Wooo-ooo' – like she's being really scary, I don't think.

'You think she's a ghost?' I said, in the same superior tone of voice she's been using on me.

'No. I'm just thinking of all the possible alternatives.'

Given some of the others, like the big sister no one ever told me about, I suppose it wasn't the worst option. But let's face it, it wasn't the most likely.

OK, I like ghost stories, but that doesn't mean I believe in ghosts. At least I don't *think* I believe in them. But I was prepared to go along with it for the time being, just to see where it was going to take her.

'OK, if she *was* a ghost,' I said, 'why would she look like me?'

'You're asking me that?' But being Nina she has to come up with some explanation. 'Maybe she's the ghost of one of your ancestors.'

'Wearing clothes like that?'

'Well, maybe she's trying to blend in. With modern life.'

'So why's she come back – like, *now*?'

'Well, maybe to warn you about something.' You have to give it to Nina; she doesn't give up easily. 'To keep you out of trouble? You said yourself she saved your life.'

'Look,' I said, 'she's not a spook, right?'

49

'Because?'

'Because . . .' I couldn't believe I was having this conversation, but it happens all the time with Nina. She acts like she's so grown up and cool and then she comes out with stuff you'd expect from your average four-year-old. And I don't mean just stuff about vampires and demons and all that – that's practically normal. These are some of the things she believes:

1) Fairieseaist. Nina believes fairies are a conquered race of pygmies who got smaller and smaller over the years and still live on in the woods and forests. They grew wings to make up for being so small.

2) Cats are from outer space. They are really aliens who are making a study of the human race. When they've finished they're going to take over and eliminate us as a danger to the rest of the universe.

3) Witches use eggshells as boats. If you don't make a hole in your boiled eggshell after you've eaten it, witches use it to sail in.

She once told me I could wash my freckles away with dew collected on the first day of May, and like an idiot I believed her. So I'm not having any nonsense from her about ghosts.

'Because they don't exist,' I said, 'and if they did exist, they wouldn't have to catch a bus.'

This shut her up. For a few seconds, at least. Then she goes: 'Well, what about the big sister thing?'

'I haven't got a big sister,' I pointed out.

'So far as you know,' Nina said.

'Excuse me?'

'Well, they might not have told you about her. She might be the skeleton in the family cupboard,' she said, looking pleased with herself.

I couldn't speak. I just shook my head.

'That could be why she's always following you and hanging about and staring at you,' she says. 'She thinks *you* look like *her*. She thinks you might be the little sister no one told *her* about. Wow. I bet that's a lot more scary for her than it is for you.' And she had a little chuckle to herself.

'Look,' I said again, 'she's not my big sister and she's not a spook – right?'

'All right.' She shrugged. 'So why do *you* think she's hanging around staring at you all the time? And saying those things to you when she got you out from under the bus, as if she knows you?'

I'd told her about that, too. I wished I hadn't

now. I gave it some thought. Maybe we *were* related. Not sisters, but distant cousins or something. Some long-lost relative.

I've hardly got any family, not that I know of. There's Mum and Dad, of course, but not many others. Dad's parents died when he was a little boy and he was brought up by his Auntie Jessie, his mother's sister, in Scotland. I've seen her a few times. She lives in a place called Kirkcudbright, which you pronounce Ker-koo-bree, in Galloway, where they've got striped pigs and cows. They call them Belted Galloways. When I told Nina this she thought it was hilarious, cos if you say someone got belted round our way it means they had too much to drink. It's also famous for being the place where they burned the last witch in Scotland.

She comes to London for Christmas – this is Auntie Jessie, not the witch – and we usually spend two weeks with her in Kirkcudbright in the summer. But she never married and she's got no kids of her own.

As for my mum, she had a mother but no father. Well, she did, of course, but she never knew him. Her mother was a single parent. She brought Mum up by herself and had nothing to do with the rest of her family. She died before I was born. But we must have some relations. Maybe the girl was a cousin or something. It could explain why she was hanging around all the time, staring at me.

We'd reached Nina's house and our car was parked outside.

'Your mum's come early for you,' said Nina.

But it wasn't my mum. It was my dad.

He was sitting in the kitchen having a cup of tea with Shella. Not so long ago I'd have run in and given him a big hug, but I didn't like to be too uncool in front of Nina, especially when she'd just been treating me like some kid, so I just stood in the kitchen doorway with my hand on my hip and I said: 'I thought you were in Russia.'

It's a funny thing but even as I did that, something really strange came over me. It was as if it was someone else talking. Someone I didn't like very much.

Shella didn't like it either. 'Don't you be such a little miss,' she says, 'and come and give your daddy a hug.'

'She's getting too big for that now,' he says. He was smiling but he looked a bit sad.

What was so stupid about all of this was that I really wanted to give him a hug. I was never sure whether he was going to come back in one piece, or in a coffin. But it was like something was holding me back. Maybe because I hated him going away so much and being so scared all the time. But he stood up and spread his arms out and I kind of walked into them with my head down. He buried his face in my hair.

'You smell of school,' he said. 'Grown-up school.'

'Yuck,' I said.

'Tell me about it,' says Nina from the hall. 'They made us run five times round the playing fields.'

'Hello, gorgeous,' he says to her, and I'm still going *yuck* inside, cos I hate it when he's like that. But Nina's all simpering, of course. Nina likes my dad, especially when he calls her gorgeous. I noticed she'd taken her glasses off. 'I hope you're keeping her out of trouble,' he says.

Her keeping *me* out of trouble . . .

'I didn't think you were coming back till next week,' I said.

'Yes, well, nothing was happening,' he said. 'So I came back to see my little girl.'

'He's back,' said Shella, 'that's the important thing. Honestly, these girls,' she said to him, 'they grow up so quick.'

'Really, mother,' says Nina, tossing her head

and doing her Scarlett O'Hara thing. When she was little she made me watch *Gone with the Wind* with her about eighteen times. 'Did you get any pictures of Putin?' she says to my dad. Putin's the Russian President. She thinks she's the only one who knows.

'I did,' said Dad. 'I got him showing off his muscles, as usual. Unfortunately, so did everyone else.'

'You need a haircut,' I said to him critically. It was practically down to his shoulders. He'll be wearing it in a ponytail next and then I'll disown him.

'And you need to learn some respect,' says Shella, glaring at me. But Dad just shrugged.

'Well, we'd better be off,' he says, finishing his tea.

It took him about ten minutes to say goodbye to Shella, who's almost as bad with him as Nina, but eventually we're sitting in the car.

'Did Mum know you were coming home?' I said, cos I was surprised she hadn't mentioned it before I went to school.

'Not until this morning,' he said. 'Didn't know it myself till last night.'

All the same, I wondered why he hadn't phoned then. Perhaps it was the time difference.

'So how's the new school?' he said as we're driving back.

'S'all right,' I said, shrugging. 'How was Russia?'

'S'all right,' he says, mimicking the way he thinks girls shrug, tossing his head about and pursing his mouth up, which was nothing like the way I'd shrugged at all.

'Go on,' I said, 'you're dying to tell me.'

'Am I?' He looked surprised. 'OK. Russia was – big. Big, brash and boring.'

'What's brash?' I said.

'In your face.'

'Sounds like Waverley,' I said.

He gave me a look. I could almost hear him thinking about this and what I meant by it. 'I remember when I went to secondary school,' he says. 'The first day they'd been mowing the grass in the school fields and they made us eat it.'

'What, the teachers?' I said.

'No, not the teachers, Dumbo – the other kids.'

'It's not quite as bad as that,' I said. Typical, I was thinking. He asks me about my school and within seconds he's telling me about his.

He looks sideways at me. 'No bullying then?'

'No.' I made it sound surprised and indignant,

as if anyone would dare. I could see he wasn't convinced.

'Well – you're not the biggest fish in the pond any more,' he said.

'What's that supposed to mean?'

'I mean, there's some real sharks in secondary school, as I recall.'

'Yeah, they're called Year Ten girls,' I said, before I could think better of it. It was just a bit of banter, but I should have kept my mouth shut.

'Give you a hard time, do they?' he says, giving me another look.

Honestly, parents. He must think I'm a right wimp.

'Not me in particular,' I said. 'They give everyone a hard time.'

'Well, get in the football team,' he said. 'Get some mates. And if that doesn't work, fight dirty.'

I'd already thought of that but it's nice to know you've got your parents behind you.

'You know any of the older girls?' he says.

I was instantly suspicious. I looked at him. 'Why d'you ask?' I said.

'Well, sometimes it helps to have an ally,' he says. 'Someone big and tough.'

'You mean like a big sister,' I said, watching him carefully.

'Yeah, sort of.' I didn't see him change colour or anything. 'Isn't there anyone you know from Pinewood?'

'Dunno,' I said. 'They change when they go to Waverley.'

'Change?' He frowned. 'In what way?'

'They dye their hair and put rings in their noses.'

I was still watching him but there was nothing. Not even a slight twitch.

'I doubt very much if they let them in Waverley looking like that,' he said. 'So what are the teachers like?'

'Boring,' I said. I thought of telling him about the one in the tracksuit who'd made us run round the playground five times, but it's not a good idea to give your parents too much information, so we didn't speak again until we got home.

I smelt it as soon as I stepped through the front door. Cooking. And there was Mum – in the kitchen – with an apron on. I stared at her.

'What?' she said.

'You're cooking,' I said.

'And?'

'Don't knock it,' said Dad, 'it might catch on.'

'Right. That's it.' Mum started to take the apron off.

'We're only joking,' says Dad. I wasn't, but still.

'I just thought that as you're home . . .' I thought for a moment she was going to burst into tears. She never could stand being teased.

Dad wrapped his arms round her and kissed her on the back of the neck. I hoped this might catch on, too.

'Sorry,' he said. 'It's Kit. She's a savage. I'll open a bottle of wine.'

So then I felt all guilty. But Mum hardly ever cooks. She leaves it all to Dad – when he's home. When he's not home we forage. That's her word for eating whatever's in the fridge or getting a takeaway. It doesn't bother me.

Dad poured a glass of wine for them both. Didn't offer me any, but it was nice watching them together for once in the kitchen.

Then Dad's phone rang.

He took it out of his pocket and looked at it.

'Aren't you going to answer it?' said Mum. I looked at her sharply cos there was something in her tone of voice I didn't quite like.

He shook his head. 'It'll be work,' he said and pressed Ignore. Mum was looking daggers at him. I ran upstairs before a row started. I've been here before. I heard Dad shouting after me.

'Don't you want a drink of something?' he said.

He obviously didn't want to be left alone with her.

'I've got homework,' I yelled. I wondered if we would get as far as sitting down at the table together. Somehow I doubted it.

I did mean to do my homework, but as I was heading for my room I passed the room we call the study, where Mum and Dad work when they're at home. I'm not exactly forbidden to enter but I know they don't like me being in there, especially Mum. But just as I'm passing the door it was like I heard this voice in my head. I know that sounds like a lame excuse but that's what it was like. I looked back over the banister. I could hear them talking in the kitchen but it didn't sound like an argument, not a real slanging match anyway. They hardly ever have slanging matches, they just sulk. I pushed open the door and went in.

Dad keeps most of his photographs on his computer now but there's a big filing cabinet next to his desk where he keeps all the contact prints he's made and

I knew there was an old family photo album in there too. He'd shown me it once, a long time ago, with pictures of him and his Auntie Jessie when he was a kid. There were even some pictures of his mum and dad. I went through the drawers one by one until I found it. There was really no reason why I shouldn't look at it, but I knew it was kind of sneaky going through his things and I didn't want to be caught in there, so I stuck it in my school bag to take back to my room where I could have a look at it in peace.

I was just about to head off when I saw another one on the shelf above Mum's desk. I didn't think I'd ever seen this one before so I climbed on a chair and took that, too. This felt even more sneaky somehow and really, whatever you think of me by now, it wasn't like me. But anyway, I snuck off back to my room with them.

I don't know what I was looking for, really. I think it was just to see if they had any relatives other than the ones I already knew about. And maybe there was someone who would look like the Girl.

I started with Dad's first. It made me all sad looking at the pictures of him as a little boy, knowing what had happened to his parents. They were in a car crash in Africa. Kenya, I think. His dad was a photographer, too – he did wildlife photographs – and they'd both gone together, leaving Dad with his Aunt Jessie. I think they were hit by a truck or something and killed outright. The first few pages were full of pictures of them, and some with my dad when he was very little. He was only three when they died. I felt so sad looking at them I nearly took the book back then and there, but I made myself keep turning the pages. And after about page four that was it: they weren't there any more.

There were pictures of him with other kids but none of them looked like they were related to him. Pictures of him at university being stupid. Pictures of him with girls. I looked at them very closely but none of them looked like they could be the Spook's mother.

It's funny thinking about your parents before they had you. I mean, they go on about it and you half listen – you know they had some kind of life before you came along – but it's hard to take it in and you never really wonder what they were like. I don't anyway. And I don't really want to know, quite honestly. It's embarrassing, your dad telling your friends what he was like when he was younger, and about getting drunk and throwing up, and music and girlfriends and stuff. As if you want to know.

But I knew he'd had them. Girlfriends, that is. He was nearly forty when he met Mum so he must have. I even knew some of their names. Suppose one of them had got pregnant and had a child? He might have a completely different family stuck away somewhere and them thinking they're the only ones. Perhaps that's why he was always away from home. He wasn't in war zones or Russia; he was with them. And when he was with us he told *them* he was in a war zone.

But was he likely to send us to the same school? I don't think so.

I put the album back in my bag and took out Mum's. There weren't so many pictures of her and she didn't seem to have any relatives apart from her mother. Rebecca, her name was, and from what I'd heard she was a bit of a rebel. She didn't get on with her parents and she left home when she was seventeen and went to live with a crowd of artists and hippies in Hastings on the south coast. She was only nineteen when she had Mum. She said the father was a local fisherman and there was never any question of them getting married. Mum thought he might have been married already.

This sounds awful, I know. I don't like to think about it, to be honest. But Mum said the two of them got on fine. They left Hastings when Mum was still quite young and went to live in London and after a while her mum got a job as an illustrator for an advertising agency. She also did some pictures for children's books. I've seen some of them. There was even one where she wrote the story, too. Mum used to read it to me when I was younger and I've still got it on my bookshelves.

It's about this mermaid who fell in love with a fisherman. So she came out of the sea and lived with him on dry land and they had a child. A little girl. But the mermaid always pined for the sea. And when her little girl was three she couldn't stand it any more, so she went back to the sea and they never saw her again. Except that sometimes at night the little girl would hear her singing. Singing lullabies to her lost daughter. And when she was seven the little girl went down to the sea one day and was never seen or heard of again. Except that sometimes the fisherman would see their shapes swimming under his boat, and at night he'd hear them both singing. *The Song of the Mermaid*, it's called.

I looked at the photographs in the album. I'd seen

them before but I hadn't been looking at anything in particular then. They were mostly of the two of them – mother and daughter – usually on holiday. They went on lots of holidays together, all over the world, even some quite adventurous ones to India and Kathmandu and South America. Her mother looked very pretty, even when she was older.

Not many other pictures, though. Just a few school ones. No one looked at all like the Spook.

I was putting them back in my bag when something slid out and fluttered down to the floor.

It was a newspaper cutting. I bent down to pick it up. And then I saw the headline.

Dulwich Fire Death
'No Accident', says Coroner

And beneath it was a photograph. She was a bit older than the pictures I'd just been looking at, but you could see it was her. My mum's mother, Rebecca. My grandmother.

6

The Fire

I picked it up as if it was going to burn my fingers and laid it carefully on the desk.

It was from the front page of the *Dulwich Herald*, dated the year before I was born. I knew from the moment I saw the headline that it was going to be bad and it was.

> The fire that claimed the life of a lonely, middle-aged woman was started deliberately, Dulwich Coroner's Court heard yesterday.
>
> The charred body of 52-year-old Ms Rebecca White was found in the burned-out ruin of her kitchen after a gas explosion which ripped through her home in Dulwich Village in

September last year.

Firemen were helpless to stop the flames from sweeping through the property and they confined their efforts to stopping the blaze from spreading to neighbouring buildings.

It was not until the following morning that they were able to enter what was left of the house where Ms White had lived alone for many years. Her body was found under layers of rubble, burned beyond recognition, and it could only be identified

The page had been roughly torn at that point and I thought at first that was all there was. I looked at the picture again. She was holding her hair and smiling. I know most people are smiling in photographs but she looked really happy and nothing like as old as fifty-two – and she certainly didn't look lonely. I wondered if Mum had taken it. It was very faded but it looked like it was at the seaside.

Then I turned over the page and saw there was more.

An investigation headed by Chief Fire Officer

Gordon Grey concluded that the cause of the blast was not a gas leak, as was first believed, but was due to the fact that all the gas taps on the stove had been turned on.

When the rising gas reached the pilot light it caused a massive explosion and the resulting fireball engulfed the house in flames.

'It's difficult to believe that every single gas tap had been turned on accidentally,' CFO Grey told the Inquest, 'and the timing of the blast – a little after midnight – makes it highly unlikely that the victim had been cooking supper.'

Then I saw my mum's name.

The victim's daughter, Ms Teresa White, 33, told the court that her mother had been diagnosed with leukaemia and there had been a recent setback in her treatment.

'She didn't want to be a nuisance to anyone,' added Ms White, who broke down in tears in the witness box. 'She was a very independent person.'

But Ms White admitted that her mother,

who had never been married, had often felt lonely and depressed.

There was more but the print seemed to be swimming in front of my eyes.

I felt like you do in football when you've been floored by some hulking great centre back and all the wind has been knocked out of you.

And yet somehow it seemed as if I'd always known. Or at least, that I'd always known there was something mysterious about the way she'd died, something that was being kept from me.

I rubbed a hand over my eyes and started reading again. But then there was a knock on the door and I heard my dad's voice asking if he could come in.

I grabbed my schoolbag and tipped all the books in it over the desk so you couldn't see the cutting. By the time Dad came in I had my head buried in a maths book.

'Doing your homework?' he said.

I stopped myself from saying something sarcastic and just grunted. Then I noticed the book was upside down and I turned it the right way round before he noticed. Fortunately he had found other things to look at.

'Wow!' he said.

I looked at him. He was standing in the doorway gazing around the room. He looked kind of stunned.

'What?' I said.

'This room,' he said.

'What about it?' I said.

'Well . . . the *mess*,' he said. Not the way my mother says it but in a kind of amazed wonder. 'It's almost – *creative*.'

At any other time I might have been annoyed but I was glad of the distraction. I didn't want him poking around among the things on my desk and finding the newspaper cutting. But at the same time I was desperate to ask him about it. Some distant memory was tugging at me, something in the back of my mind, and I was sure it had something to do with my dad.

'Was there something you wanted?' I said.

'I just came to see if I could help you with your homework.' But he was still looking round the room like some explorer who's battled through oceans and jungles and over mountain ranges and stumbled into the lost city of the Amazons, only to find it's a dump.

'What's *that*?' he said.

I followed the direction of his gaze.

'A rickshaw,' I said.

It was something Nina gave me. From one of her uncles in Lahore. They're always bringing her things and she's always giving them away. Usually to me. She says she doesn't want them cluttering up her room. She doesn't mind them cluttering up mine, cos she says it's such a tip anyway. I'm supposed to give them back when one of the uncles comes to stay, but she's forgotten who gave her what. This is a three-wheeled motor rickshaw. Nina says they use them as taxis in Lahore but this is about a quarter the size of the real ones. It's still pretty big though. I don't know how her uncle got it on the plane. We had to take it to pieces to get it through my bedroom door. Nina says her uncle drove it to England, but that's ridiculous, cos he'd never have got into it. All Nina's uncles are enormous. It's made of tin and all the panels are painted with views of the Himalayas. Not that you can see them, not with all my clothes draped over it.

'What's it for?' Dad's staring at it like it's going to bite him.

'It's for riding round in,' I said. 'Nina put her dolls in it but then she decided it wasn't cool.'

'Oh,' he said vaguely.

He's looking round the room again. 'Where are *your* dolls?' he says.

'They're under the bed,' I told him, 'in a suitcase.'

'Why?' he frowned.

I can't believe this. Why are we talking about *dolls*? I've just discovered my grandmother killed herself and we're talking about dolls.

'What do you mean – *why*?' I asked him.

'Well, I mean, where are they going?'

'They're not going anywhere,' I said. 'They're dolls.'

'So . . .' He shook his head. 'I'm sorry, but . . . why the suitcase?'

'I just didn't want to throw them away.' I was going to start screaming soon. I was going to start throwing things.

'OK,' he said, but he still sounded puzzled. 'But – aren't you supposed to play with them?'

'What?' I said. Honestly, I felt like I was drowning. I needed air.

'You know – dress them up and things. Have tea parties.'

'Dad,' I said. 'I don't play with dolls. I'm nearly twelve.'

'You're not!' He looked astonished. Dad's funny

about time. He doesn't really understand it. Sometimes he talks to me as if I'm grown up and sometimes it's as if I'm about two and a half. He's still looking round the room like he's trying to remember when he last came in here. He doesn't come into my room much; I'll say that for him. He believes in giving people some privacy, not like Mum. But he's been here plenty of times since the dolls went away and never said anything.

He wandered around the room peering at things. I tried to concentrate on the maths book.

A rectangular football pitch is 65 metres by 100 metres. A footballer runs once round the perimeter of the pitch. How far does he run?

'You've still got the hamster cage,' Dad says.

'Yes,' I said.

'Can't you bring yourself to get rid of that either?'

The hamster died a year ago. He was called Hammy. At least that's what I called him. Dad called him Houdini, cos he kept escaping. There was this little hatch in the top of the cage and he used to stand on the platform under it and push it open like a weightlifter. It had a really strong spring on it, but it didn't stop him. When he escaped he used to go into Mum and Dad's bedroom and climb up the curtains.

I guess he was trying to get out of the window, or maybe he just liked climbing curtains. The scrabbling noises he made woke Mum up and if Dad wasn't there she'd yell for me to come and catch him, cos she couldn't bear to pick him up. She said it was like picking up a rat. She found one of Dad's weights from his barbells and put it on top of the hatch to stop him from getting out, but he could push that off, too. You'd find the weight lying on the floor and the cage empty.

If he didn't climb the curtains he hid behind the books in the bookshelves in the living room. He'd stay there for days in the space between the back of the books and the back of the shelves. You'd know he was there because every now and then he'd push a book out. You'd be sitting there watching television and suddenly a book would pop out and fall to the floor. Mum said it was like having a poltergeist. We never knew why he did this, or why he picked on certain books instead of others. Dad made a list of the titles and said he didn't like girly books or books without proper endings. I just think he got bored.

Then one day he died.

They told me he'd escaped again and this time he'd made it to the world outside.

I knew it wasn't true. I knew he never really wanted to get past the curtains, or to the end of the tunnel behind the books.

That was when I put out the appeal on Twitter, but I knew in my heart of hearts that he was dead. The trouble was I didn't know *how* he'd died.

Why do parents think they're protecting you when they don't tell you the truth about someone dying? It can never be worse than you imagine.

I'd lie awake at night thinking that he'd got into the washing machine and been washed to death. Or torn to pieces in the food mixer. Or sucked into the vacuum machine when Mum vacuumed the curtains.

Well, now I had something else to worry about.

'You saving his cage for the next one?' Dad said.

'I just haven't got round to throwing that out, either,' I said. This was a lie. The real reason was I couldn't bear to, just in case he came back some day. Or we found him hibernating in the bookshelves.

'I'm too old for hamsters,' I said.

'Too old for hamsters, too old for dolls,' said Dad. 'What about boys?'

I ignored him. He was just trying to provoke me. He ambled over to my desk and stood behind me, peering at the books I'd tipped over it.

'This your homework?' he said.

'Yes,' I said. I was really tense now in case he picked the maths book up and saw what was under it.

'What is it?'

'Maths,' I said. 'Key Stage Three.'

Then he saw the photo albums.

'What you doing with these?' he said, reaching for them.

'We've got a project,' I said, 'on The Family.'

It just came to me, like that – as a way of explaining why I had the albums – but suddenly I saw it had other possibilities.

'Oh yes?' He took the albums over to the bed and sat down with them.

'Like who my grandparents were and what they did and all that,' I told him, making it up as I went along. 'Like a family tree.'

'Oh yes?'

'I'm supposed to interview them. My grandparents. But I can't, can I, cos they're all dead.'

'I suppose you can't – no.' He's browsing through the book, turning the pages, not really listening.

'I haven't really got a family, have I?' I said.

'You've got me and your mum,' he says.

'Yes – but . . .'

'And your Auntie Jessie.'

'I haven't really got time to go up to Scotland,' I said, meaning it to be sarcastic. 'Isn't there anyone a bit closer I can interview?'

'What do you mean?'

'Haven't I got any cousins or anything I don't know about? Living in London?'

'Don't think so. Your mum might have, but we've never met any of 'em. Good grief. Look at me at uni – was I ever that young?'

'I saw somebody who looked like me the other day,' I said casually. 'I thought we might be related.'

'Oh yes? Where was that?' He didn't sound very interested. He was still looking at the pictures of himself.

'At school,' I said. 'She could have been my older sister.'

He shook his head. 'Can't be one of mine. I drowned them soon as they were born. Didn't want any more like you.'

There was a shout from downstairs. Supper was ready.

'Food!' he says. 'Real food! Race you downstairs.'

7

Back from the Dead

'What's up with you?' Nina says to me when she sees my face in the morning. I'd seen it myself in the bathroom mirror: all white and pinched with dark marks under my eyes like bruises. 'You look terrible,' she says, peering at me. 'You haven't seen the Spook again?'

I shook my head. I had another spook to worry about now. I'd hardly slept all night. When I did sleep I had terrible dreams about my grandmother and the fire. I'd be standing outside the house watching the smoke and the flames and I'd see her face in an upstairs window, her hands pressed against the glass and her mouth open in a soundless scream. It wasn't just that she was burning to death. It was as if she was trying to tell me something before she died, but I couldn't hear her and I couldn't do anything to save her.

The other dream I remembered was just after the fire and I was stumbling through the ruins of the burned-out house. The ashes were still hot and the air was thick with smoke. And then I stumbled on her body. Her charred body, as the paper said. Her head was just a blackened skull with sockets where the eyes had been and her jaw was locked open as wide as it would go as if she'd been screaming when she died. And the rest of her looked just like a piece of charcoal.

Everyone said I had a powerful imagination, but in my dreams I had no control over it. It took me over completely.

I'd spent half the night lying in the dark terrified to go back to sleep because I knew she'd be waiting for me with her blackened skull and her empty eye sockets and her scream.

But I didn't want to tell Nina that I'd just found out my grandmother had killed herself. Not yet anyway – and probably not ever.

I was in a foul mood all morning. Miss Bishop told me off for not finishing my maths homework and then gave me a detention for muttering at her. My first detention. An hour after school on Tuesday. Not that I cared. It was better than being at home.

'This place is driving me mental,' I said to Nina during lunch break. 'A detention for muttering! You'd think we were in prison.'

'It would have been more than detention if she'd heard what you muttered,' Nina pointed out.

This was true.

'You should have told her your dad had just got back from Russia,' said Nina. 'And you couldn't really shut yourself away doing homework.'

'I didn't think of that,' I said.

'So did you have a nice evening?' she says. This wasn't as innocent as it sounds. She knew Mum and Dad were having problems. If she hadn't heard it from me she'd probably heard it from Shella, even if Shella didn't know she was listening. There wasn't much you could keep from Nina.

I shrugged. I didn't want to tell her about Mum and Dad either. But then it all came out.

We'd sat round the table with Dad going on about how wonderful the food was and Mum just sitting there not saying a word and pushing it round the plate with her fork and then afterwards she stomps off upstairs and he sits watching television by himself. His first night home after two weeks. And I'm in my room, not doing my maths homework. Happy families.

'Is that all?' Nina says. 'I thought you were going to say they'd been screaming at each other all night.'

'It would have been better if they had,' I said. 'It's the silence I can't stand. And when they do speak they're so polite to each other, it's like they've only just met. If anyone's going to be screaming it's me.'

'I wish my parents were polite to each other,' Nina said. 'You should hear the way they go on. You'd think they were in EastEnders. I think they might get divorced.'

I knew Nina was only saying this to make me feel better. Nina knew her mum and dad weren't going to get divorced. She knew they loved each other. Nina can be a pain at times but she's a good friend. She even came to watch the football trials and she hates football.

I thought it was going to be a disaster. I was playing out of position and the whole of the first half I played like a zombie.

When we came off at half time we were two-nil down and I was in a worse mood than ever.

'I thought you played quite well,' Nina said. 'You nearly scored a goal.'

'Yes – in my own net,' I snarled at her. 'You're supposed to score goals against the other team, not your own. Duh.'

I'd nearly given away a penalty too and I'd hardly made one good pass all game. But then in the second half they let me play much further up field and I started to turn it on. A couple of minutes in I put Michelle clear through on goal with a beautiful long ball from the halfway line. She shot straight at the keeper, but it did a lot for my confidence, even if it did nothing for hers. A few minutes later I picked up a loose ball from a corner and found Michelle's head at the far post. This time even she couldn't miss.

From then on I couldn't do anything wrong. I had another assist for the equalizer and then about a minute into stoppage time I picked up a long ball from defence and took it right through on my own and chipped over the goalie for the winner. I came off the pitch feeling like Lionel Messi. Nina had gone home, of course, but I hadn't expected her to stay the whole ninety minutes; I was amazed she'd stayed until half time.

I hate to admit it but it was a better game for being

girls only, certainly for me. Girls tend to stay on their feet more. They don't throw themselves into tackles and you get a lot more time on the ball. It's far more of a passing game, a positional game, and that suits my style of play. And you're not forever worrying about someone smashing into you seconds after you've passed to someone.

They don't tell you straight away, but I knew there had to be a strong chance of making the first team.

And then suddenly everything's all right. And not just on the football field. When I go home that night it's a completely different atmosphere. Mum had bought Dad a haggis, which is one of his favourite meals. In case you don't know – well you won't want to know, but I'll tell you anyway – it's a sheep's bladder stuffed with minced meat and onions and you eat it with mashed turnip and potatoes, which Dad calls neeps and tatties. Gross. He says his Auntie Jessie used to make it for him in Kirkcudbright. Mum and I had shepherd's pie, which he says is exactly the same without the sheep's bladder, but that's like saying a fish head's the same as fish and chips. Fish head and chips. I don't think it would work, do you? Well, it might work in Kirkcudbright.

All through the meal they're laughing and joking

with each other and then they curled up on the sofa together to watch some crappy Italian detective series. I wanted to watch 'A Question of Sport' but I didn't say anything, I just sat there trying to follow it. Then they started kissing and I had to leave the room. But it was worth it to see them happy together.

I even started to enjoy school. I mean the schoolwork, not just the football. Well, maybe not *enjoy* it, but I felt I was getting on top of it. They have a whole different way of teaching at secondary school. Mostly it's all curriculum but sometimes they do something really interesting. Like in the literature hour Miss Prentice did fairy tales. At first I thought she'd flipped. She was like my dad; she thought we were still six. But she did the *meaning* of fairy tales. Or the different meanings. She made us think about them. Like in *Little Red Riding Hood*, she says, 'So why does the mother send her little girl off into the forest if it's so dangerous?'

She watched us thinking about that.

'So – you're saying the mother *wants* her to get killed by the wolf?' says Nina.

'Not consciously,' says Miss Prentice. 'But maybe *un*consciously – yes. It's a possibility.'

'But why?' said Nina.

84

'Think about it. Why do you think? Mothers and daughters. Not always an easy relationship. Maybe the mother's a bit jealous. Maybe the father's been paying the daughter too much attention and not paying any to his wife. Maybe the daughter's a bit of a princess.'

I knew she didn't mean a real princess; she meant like Nina.

'But she wouldn't want her to be killed by a wolf,' Nina says. I knew she'd be taking this personally.

'Not *consciously*, maybe,' says Miss Prentice.

It's like there's just the two of them having a little heart-to-heart, and the rest of us are sitting there trying to follow it. Like me with the Italian detective series. But actually, I was quite interested in this.

'But anyway, whatever she wants, she sends her off into the forest,' says Miss Prentice, 'telling her not to leave the path. So why *does* she leave the path?'

'Because her mother told her not to,' I said.

'Thank you, Kit,' says Miss Prentice when everyone's stopped laughing. 'That's one reason. Any others?'

There were a few others. She wants to gather wild flowers to give to her grandmother. There was a bird with a broken wing. She wants to have a pee.

Miss Prentice listens to these patiently. And then she says, 'And what if she *wants* to meet the wolf? What if she's bored? What if she wants something more in her life than running errands for her mother? What if she wants a bit of excitement, a bit of danger even? What if she wants a bit of *fun*?'

Personally, I think Miss Prentice was talking about herself.

She could see we weren't convinced. 'So let me ask you this,' she says. 'Why does she tell the wolf where she's going? Why does she say she's on her way to her grandmother's – a sick old lady who lives alone in the forest? I mean, is she stupid or something? Or does she actually *want* to destroy her own family?'

'Why would she want to do that?' This was somebody else for a change. A girl called Lucy Mandela.

'Because the family is like a prison for her,' says Miss Prentice. 'Because she wants to set herself free.' She gazes around at us and we're all staring back at her, even the headbangers – wondering if this is for real or she's having a laugh. 'The wolf is a symbol of subversion,' she says. She can see that at least half the class doesn't have the faintest idea what she's talking about. 'Destruction, if you like. All the things that can destroy the happy home. Family, tradition, society as we know it. But all human progress requires some level of destruction – or dissolution. Think about it.' She beams at us brightly.

Then she goes on to give us her take on *Cinderella*, *Puss in Boots*, *Bluebeard* and *Hansel and Gretel*. According to Miss Prentice they're all warnings. Don't trust your parents. Don't trust any adult. They're all out to get you.

'Even teachers?' says Nina.

'*Especially* teachers,' says Miss Prentice, smiling.

By the time she's finished we're thinking everything we've ever been told is lies and everyone over the age of thirty wants us to get lost in a forest and die.

'Have a good day,' says Miss Prentice smugly when the bell goes for lunch break and we run screaming out into the playground.

That night I come home and the wolf's back.

I don't know what's caused it, whether somebody said something or did something or what, but it had to be something serious. Mum's brewing up a Force Ten Sulk and Dad's grinding his teeth so you can actually hear them, like boulders in a glacier.

Honestly, I don't know how it happens. There was no sign of it before I went to school. They weren't exactly laughing and hugging but they seemed quite relaxed with each other. They even had a joke about the muesli at breakfast. Dad said there weren't enough nuts in it and Mum said there were nuts enough in the house with me and him. It wasn't much of a joke. I mean, we didn't exactly split our sides, but it was halfway to being classed as banter. Then I come home and it's like a lockdown at the jailhouse.

If I hadn't been in Year Seven I'd have said an evil witch had cast a spell on them. But I knew what Miss Prentice would say. She'd say the witch was the outward expression of inner discontent. A symbol of their desire to escape the bonds of matrimony. Or something like that.

I was glad to escape to my room and get on with my homework. The early Middle Ages. The Viking invasions. They were murdering and looting and ravishing all over England, according to the book I was reading. Churches and monasteries were burned to the ground. Monks and priests were hung up by their heels over burning altars. No one was safe, not even the dead. They dug open the graves so they could steal all the gold and jewellery that was buried with the corpses. All the men were put to the sword and the women and children led into captivity. No more happy families. England was a wasteland.

Bring on the Vikings, I thought. I was in that kind of a mood.

Next day there was climbing practice. After school, that is. On the climbing wall at the local leisure centre. I usually looked forward to it, but today I wasn't in the mood. I was trudging along with my head down, thinking that if I had a serious fall and smashed my head in maybe it would teach them a lesson. Mum and Dad that is. I imagined lying in hospital in a coma while they sat by my bedside wishing they hadn't been such a pain. Then I looked up and saw the Spook.

It was the first time in more than a week. She was standing at the bus stop the same as last time, wearing her school uniform. There was a whole herd of Year Ten girls at the bus stop, but she didn't seem to be with them. At least she wasn't talking to any of them, and she was standing a little apart. I remember thinking that was a bit odd. I knew she was foul-mouthed and her face was covered with bits of sticking plaster and she'd got a death's-head moth tattooed on her right shoulder but that doesn't exactly make you an outsider with Year Ten girls.

Then I saw the bus coming and on a sudden impulse I ran across the road and joined the queue. I don't know why. I think I had some idea of stalking her, like she'd been stalking me. Or maybe deep down I was wondering if she was real or whether she'd suddenly vanish and then I'd know for certain that she was all in my mind.

She seemed real enough. She was standing about four or five girls in front of me and I saw that she had earphones on. Ghosts don't have earphones. Not in any books I've read. Nor do they ride on buses. It was a double-decker and she flashed her pass at the driver and headed upstairs.

I went downstairs and sat where I had a clear view of people getting on and off. We were going in the opposite direction from the leisure centre, but I thought so long as we didn't go too far I could probably still get back in time for climbing practice. I wanted to find out where she lived.

The journey went on and on. We were travelling along the South Circular but I had no idea where we were. Girls from our school were getting off at every stop but not her. Maybe she *had* vanished, I thought. I was wondering about going up to the top deck to look, and then suddenly she's standing there waiting to get off at the next stop.

I hung back until the last moment and then just before the doors closed I jumped off after her. She headed off down a side road and I waited until she'd got a fair bit ahead of me and then followed. She was still plugged into her earphones and I trailed a fair way behind her on the opposite side of the road. It wasn't an area I knew. The houses were quite big and solid, probably Victorian, and they were set back from the street with long front gardens. The outer fringes of suburbia, I thought, remembering what Nina had said. But it certainly wasn't emo or goth territory.

The sun had slipped down behind the rooftops but it was a mild autumn evening, almost summery. There was a smell of smoke, as if someone was burning leaves, but there was no one else about. Once the girl stopped and I bent down and pretended to be tying my shoe laces. I don't know what I'd have said if she'd spotted me and asked me what I was doing there. I couldn't pretend I lived there because I didn't know where it was. Besides, she *knew* where I lived. But after a moment she walked on. I'd just started to follow her again when she turned into one of the drives and I lost her behind the trees in the front garden.

I ran to catch up and then slowed down again and walked along the opposite side of the road, glancing casually towards the house she'd gone into. She was standing in the driveway and there was someone walking across the lawn towards her. A tall, thin woman with straggly grey hair, slightly mad-looking. It looked like she'd been doing some gardening. She had a pair of shears in her hands and the smell of burning was stronger, though I couldn't see a fire.

Then suddenly the girl turned round and stared straight at me. It stopped me dead in my tracks. It wasn't just that she'd seen me – it was something about her. Her expression, maybe. She looked so like me. She didn't look surprised to see me. I think she must have known all along that I'd been following her. It was as if she'd led me here.

Then I saw the face of the woman who was with her. And that was the real shocker. It almost stopped my heart in its tracks.

It was the face of the woman who had been burned to death in a house fire a year before I was born.

The face of my grandmother.

8

Things That Go Bump in the Night

The woman smiled at me and raised her arm as if beckoning me to join them. And that broke the spell. I started to run. In a blind panic, as if my life depended on it. I ran until I couldn't run any more. Then I walked. I had no idea where I was or where I was going. I just wanted to get away from that place as fast as possible.

Finally I came out on a main road and saw a bus coming along, so I jumped on it. I didn't know where it was going; I didn't particularly care. It took me to Streatham and from there I caught another bus home. It was far too late by then to go to the leisure centre, and in any case I was too shook up to even think about climbing walls.

No sign of Dad, but Mum shouts down to me from upstairs.

'Is that you, Kit? I'm just finishing something off. How'd the climbing go?'

'I fell off the wall and broke my leg,' I said.

'Great,' she says, 'I'll be down in a minute.'

I knew she wouldn't, of course. Not when she's 'just finishing something off'. It can take hours. I thought about talking to her about what I'd just seen, but I wouldn't know where to start.

I tried to Skype Nina but she wasn't answering. So I had another restless night trying to make sense of it all. When I did sleep I had terrible nightmares about the fire. I even had one where I was a witch and I was being burned alive at the stake. It was so vivid I even remember my hair catching fire.

Next day was a Saturday. No school. I went round to Nina's as soon as I'd had breakfast and told her everything. The story in the newspaper about the fire, the picture of my grandmother, the suicide verdict – and then what had happened on my way home from school.

One thing I'll say for Nina; she's very good in a crisis. She listens to you very carefully and then she asks the kind of questions that make you realize that no matter how bad you thought things were, they're really much, much worse.

First she wanted to know exactly where the house was, but of course I couldn't tell her. I'd been in such a blind panic I hadn't noticed the house number or the name of the street or anything.

'But you were close enough to see her face?' Nina says.

I nodded.

'So what are you saying? That your grandmother didn't die? That it was someone else's body they found?'

'That's what I thought,' I said. 'At first. But, Nina, she hadn't *aged*.'

Nina didn't get it.

'She looked exactly the same as she did in the photograph,' I told her. 'And that was more than twelve years ago.'

She got it now. But I have to say she took it very calmly. A lot more calmly than I had. 'So. OK.' I can see her thinking about it, trying to come up with what she calls a rational explanation. This is a girl who believes in fairies and who smashes her eggshells so witches don't use them to sail in. 'So did she have a younger sister?'

'No. I'm sure I'd have known about it,' I said. 'Why would they not tell me?'

'They didn't tell you she killed herself,' Nina pointed out.

This was true. 'But she'd have to be my nan's twin,' I said. 'An identical twin.'

'Who hasn't aged.'

'Exactly.'

'So we're talking about another spook?'

I said nothing.

'Well, the only other explanation is that you imagined it,' she said.

Of course I'd wondered about that. But I couldn't believe I'd imagined all of it. The girl, the bus journey, a woman who looks exactly like my dead grandmother . . . I mean, *why*?

'Do you *believe* in ghosts?' Nina asks me curiously, as if she's conducting a survey.

'No,' I said. 'I mean, I don't know. I thought I didn't but . . . Do you?'

'It mentions them in the Koran,' said Nina cautiously. 'At least, they're a kind of ghost. They're called jinn.'

'Jim?' I said, puzzled. 'What – all of them?'

'No. *Jinn*.' Nina rolled her eyes. She spelled it for me. 'But they're not ghosts of dead people. At least I don't think so.'

'So what are they?'

'They're evil spirits who come up from Hell to tempt you into doing bad things.'

'D'you think that's what these are?'

'Could be. But I think they only pick on Muslims. I'll have to ask Dad.'

'Don't you dare!' I panicked. 'He'll think I've gone completely mental.'

'He thinks that already,' Nina assured me. 'It won't make any difference.'

'Even so, you're not to tell him. Or anyone,' I warned her. 'This is between you and me.'

'OK, OK, no need to freak out.' Nina reached for her laptop. 'Let's see what Google has to say.'

Google had quite a lot to say about ghosts. Ghosts – otherwise known as phantoms, ghouls, spooks, wraiths, apparitions and about half a dozen things I'd never even heard of – could be explained by quite a number of things, but the traditional belief was that they were the spirits of the dead who could appear in one form or another to the living.

'"Ghosts are generally described as solitary essences

that haunt particular locations, objects, or people they were associated with in life,"' Nina read out. "'They can be invisible presences that are sensed or heard – things that go bump in the night – or barely visible, wispy shapes hanging in the air, or realistic, life-like visions.

"'Ghosts in the classical world often appeared in the form of vapour or smoke, but at other times they were described as being substantial, appearing as they had been at the time of death, complete with the wounds that killed them" – or with rings through their noses and horrible tattoos with skulls and moths and . . .'

I grabbed the computer and angled the screen so I could see it too. It's never safe to trust what Nina reads out to you because she's just as likely to have made it up herself. But this time she'd only made up the last bit.

"'The spirit of the dead was believed to hover near the place where it had died or been buried,"' I read. "'Belief in ghosts is characterized by the recurring fear of the returning dead, who may harm the living, such as the Romanian or Serbian *vampir*."'

Nina's eyes gleamed. She loves vampires. 'Maybe she's a vampire,' she said. 'She didn't bite you, did she, when she knocked you off your bike?'

'She didn't knock me off my bike . . .' I started to say but she was peering at my neck looking for bites. I pushed her away.

'Nina, she is not a vampire.'

'Why not? She *looked* like a vampire, the way you first described her, like one of the Year Ten girls – and if you ask me, they're *all* vampires. And that moth you think you saw on her shoulder – it could have been a bat. Look up vampires.'

She reached for the mouse but I knocked her hand out of the way and we carried on reading about ghosts.

There was a lot of stuff about ghosts in different countries and cultures and religions. The ancient Greeks, it said, held annual feasts to which ghosts were invited in order to 'honour and placate them'. Then after the meal was over they would be firmly told to leave until the same time next year.

'Next time you see her maybe you should invite her to dinner,' Nina said.

'Yeah, great. Dinner at our house. That would work. She'd never want to come back. Not next year, not ever.'

Nina gave me a funny look, but I didn't want

to tell her about that stuff. I wanted to know more about ghosts.

We read about the so-called rational explanations. Like something called the 'Stone Tape' theory. According to this, ghosts were 'collections of energy' stored in the stones of certain places where bad things had happened, and then 'transmitted' like a video. Or else they were 'telepathic hallucinations that emanate from the subconscious mind' – usually when people are stressed out by something.

'Are you stressed out by anything?' Nina asked innocently.

'Yes, I'm stressed out by you,' I said. 'But I've been stressed out by you since pre-school playgroup and I've never seen ghosts before.'

On the whole I didn't find the 'rational' explanations any more convincing than the spiritual ones.

Nina was looking thoughtful. 'The times you saw her,' she began slowly, like she's given up on the law and now she's a psychiatrist, 'were you feeling particularly anxious about anything?'

I pretended to think about it. 'Well, when I fell off my bike in front of the bus,' I said, 'I *was* quite anxious, yes.'

'OK,' she said. 'That's understandable.' She doesn't always get sarcasm, Nina. 'And the next time you saw her, a bus came into that, too, didn't it?'

'No,' I said. 'The next time was on the Common with Omar. And the time after that was outside my window. I can't remember seeing any buses.'

'But that was the same day. When it was still fresh in your mind. The next time – when I was with you – you saw her standing at a bus stop.'

'Ye-es, but—'

'And the time after that was also at a bus stop. And you followed her onto the bus.'

'So what are you trying to say? You think I'm haunted by a bus?'

'I didn't say that.'

'No, no, I think you might have something here. It would be a first, as far as I know, but . . .'

'If you're going to be silly about it . . .'

'Sorry. Go on.'

'I'm not saying you're haunted by a bus. But the sight of a bus – after what happened – might bring it all back to you.'

'Bring what back?'

'The memory of lying in the road with the bus coming at you.'

'Ah, so you believe that *did* happen? I didn't imagine that bit?'

'I'll come back to that. But just for now, let's focus on the bus.'

'OK, I'm focusing on the bus.' I let my eyes go crossed and stared at a point about six centimetres in front of my nose.

'Was it the same bus as the one that nearly ran you over?'

'I can't remember. I didn't notice the number.'

'But you know what stop it was?'

So we stopped looking up ghosts and looked up the London bus routes.

The stuff on ghosts was easier to understand. Even Nina was baffled and she's good on bus routes. We followed the routes along the South Circular, going east from Tooting with Nina calling out the names.

'Streatham, Streatham Hill, Norwood Road, West Dulwich, Dulwich Village . . .'

'That's where my grandmother lived,' I said.

'Where?'

'Dulwich Village. According to the newspaper.'

'So − could that have been where you got off the bus?'

'I don't know. But the house was burned to the ground.'

'Maybe it was rebuilt,' said Nina. 'And now it's haunted.'

'What – by the ghost of my grandmother?'

Nina looked up haunted houses.

'"A place where ghosts are reported is described as haunted,"' she read.

'Brilliant,' I said. 'Who writes this stuff?'

'"Supernatural activity inside such places is said to be mainly associated with violent or tragic events in the building's past – such as murder, accidental death, or suicide."'

We looked at each other.

'Now we're getting somewhere,' said Nina. She read on:

'"Many cultures and religions believe the essence of a being continues to exist. Some people argue that the 'spirits' of those who have died have not 'passed over' and are trapped inside the property where their memories and energy are strongest."'

'I don't think I want to read any more,' I said. I felt a bit sick to tell the truth.

But Nina felt she was on to something now. You couldn't stop her. It's the lawyer in her.

'"These spirits may be looking for atonement for sins they have committed in life – or *revenge on people who caused them to suffer in life . . .*" Whoops.'

'What do you mean, "Whoops"?' I said.

'Well, think about it. If these *are* ghosts, why have they been appearing to you?'

'But I haven't done anything to them,' I protested. 'What have I done to them? I mean, my grandmother died before I was born.'

'Well, maybe she's trying to tell you something. Maybe she wants you to help her get revenge on somebody else.'

'Like who?'

'Like whoever killed her.'

'But she killed herself.'

'According to the inquest.'

'You think somebody murdered her?'

'Maybe. Maybe that's what she's trying to tell you. Maybe she's trying to lead you to who it was.'

'But what about the girl?'

'I don't know. Maybe she's the *spirit guide*,' she said. 'The ghost that leads you to the place where evil was done.'

Then I told her what was really worrying me, deep down. 'What if she's *my* ghost. I mean, the ghost of *me*.'

She stares at me. 'How can she be *your* ghost, numptie? You're still alive. At least I think you are.' She reached out and pinched my arm. Hard.

'That hurt,' I yelled. 'Why'd you do that?'

'Just to make sure you're real, and not a figment of my imagination.'

'Yeah? How about if I kick you? Then you'll know for sure.' I lashed out with my right foot and caught her neatly on the ankle.

So now she's hopping about on one leg and moaning that she's going to tell my dad that I kicked her.

'You deserved it,' I said.

'I'm only trying to be helpful,' she scowled at me. 'If you don't want me to analyse this for you . . .'

'No, please, go on,' I said. 'You're making me feel a lot better. Analyse away.'

'Well, all I'm saying is, how can she be *your* ghost if you're still alive?'

'That's the point,' I said. 'That's what I've been thinking about. She's about three years older than me, isn't she?'

'If you say so.'

'So?'

'So what?'

'So ghosts don't age, do they? Not so far as we know. They stay the same age as when they died. So what does that tell you?'

'Go on.'

'How about – I'm going to die at the same age the Spook is now?'

'That's ridiculous,' said Nina. But she didn't look too sure.

I grabbed the mouse off her and clicked back on ghosts. There was something I'd seen earlier, something I hadn't really wanted to take in.

'"The appearance of a ghost has often been thought of as an ill omen",' I read. '"Seeing one's own ghostly double, or doppelgänger, is a sign of impending death."'

She was silent for a moment. I could see it had shaken her. But only for a moment.

'But she's not your ghostly double,' she almost yelled at me. 'She's an emo!'

'So maybe that's what I'm going to become.'

'Wow!' She put her head back and stared at me and blinked a couple of times, like she was trying to imagine it.

'I'm going to become an emo and then I'm going

to die,' I said. 'I'm not sure what's worse, really.'
I was trying to be cool. 'But personally I'd put it a bit
stronger than Wow.'

9

The Doppelgänger Effect

'You're not going to die,' said Nina firmly. But I could tell she was more worried than she sounded. 'I mean, the first time you saw her, she saved your life. Why would she do that if she's a, what did you call it, "a sign of impending death?"'

I'd been thinking about this and I thought I had the answer.

'Because if I died now, she wouldn't exist.'

'But she *doesn't* exist, not according to you. She's a ghost!'

'I mean, she wouldn't exist *as a ghost*.'

'I'm sorry, you've lost me,' said Nina, shaking her head.

I struggled to stay calm. 'If I died now, just before

I was twelve, she couldn't possibly exist as a fifteen-year-old ghost, could she?'

'Couldn't she?'

'No,' I almost screamed at her. 'Because *ghosts don't age*. They stay the same age as when they died. Are you with me yet?'

'Er, can I get back to you on that?'

'You're useless,' I said, picking up my bag.

'No, hang on,' says Nina. 'I'm sorry. I know what you're talking about, but what I can't understand is what makes you think this ghost is *you*?'

'I can see myself in her,' I said. 'Don't ask me how. I just can.'

'Let's just consider the alternatives,' she said patiently, like she's Miss Prentice off on one of her theories about *Little Red Riding Hood*.

'Go on.' I sat down again.

'Well, she could just be a girl in Year Ten – a real, *live* girl in Year Ten – who looks a bit like you.'

'So how come we've never seen her around?'

'But you *have* seen her. That's the whole point, isn't it?'

'Yes. But *you* haven't. And I haven't actually seen her at school. Not with other kids. Or any of the teachers. Not actually talking to them or playing games or, or . . .' I thought of other things girls in Year Ten did . . . 'Or kicking seven colours of the rainbow out of someone.'

'Well, it's a big school. I mean, there's seven or eight classes in each year. That's two or three hundred kids.'

'I suppose so,' I said. I wanted to believe it. I wanted to believe anything except that I'd just seen my doppelgänger and I was going to die.

'Let's ask Omar,' says Nina, jumping up off the bed.

I panicked. 'Ask Omar what?'

I didn't want to get into a discussion with Omar about my ghostly double. He'd think I was a total freak.

'Omar's in Year Ten,' Nina reminded me. 'He might know her.'

'But what will we tell him?' I said.

Nina thought about it. 'We'll tell him she stole your phone and we want to get it back.'

This seemed reasonable enough.

'Nothing about ghosts?'

'Nothing about ghosts,' she said.

We found Omar downstairs in the kitchen in his dressing gown. It was eleven o'clock and he was having breakfast and reading the sports pages.

'Omar,' says Nina, taking the paper off him. 'We want to talk to you.'

'I was reading that,' said Omar. He made a grab for it, but Nina held it out of his reach.

'It won't take a minute,' she said. 'We just want to ask you something.'

He stood up. 'Nina, give me the paper back,' he said. His tone was menacing. I thought this was only going to end one way. But I was wrong.

'You want me to tell Mum about Rose Tully?' Nina said.

Omar glared at her for a moment. Then he sat down again.

Who was Rose Tully? I wondered. And what could Nina tell their mum about her and Omar?

'We only want to talk to you for a minute,' Nina said in a reasonable tone of voice.

'What about?'

'Kit thinks she's seen a ghost and we want to know if it's in your year.'

'What?' He looked from her to me and shook his head. Now I was glaring at her. She was going to get it when we were alone.

'Only joking,' she said. 'But there's this girl at our

school; we think she's in Year Ten and she looks a bit spooky.'

'They all look a bit spooky,' said Omar. 'Anyway, what about her?'

'Kit thinks she stole her phone.'

Omar looked at me. 'Have you lost your new phone?' He sounded sympathetic.

I could feel myself blushing. 'I think so,' I said. In fact, it was in the pocket of my hoodie. I wished I'd switched it off. What if it suddenly started ringing?

'And you think this girl in Year Ten took it?'

'She might have,' Nina answered for me. 'Tell him what she looked like,' she said to me, winking.

'Well, she's got hair about the same colour as mine,' I said, 'only a bit longer and tattier, and she's very pale and freckled and spotty. And she's got sticking plasters covering the holes in her ears and her nose.'

'That's when she's at school,' explained Nina.

'And when she's not at school?'

'She's an emo.'

'Figures. And what does she look like when she's an emo?'

'Well, the times I saw her, she had choppy blonde hair with a red streak at the front, and very heavy chalk-white make-up with black lipstick and a ring through her nose, another ring through her right eyebrow and three through one ear.'

'And a death's-head moth tattooed on her left shoulder,' put in Nina.

Omar was starting to look a bit haunted himself.

'And she swears a lot,' I said, 'and has a kind of swagger, like you don't want to mess with her – and if you give her the slightest bit of bother she'll put the boot in.'

'That narrows the field a bit,' Omar said. But he was being sarcastic. He gets a lot of stick from the Year Ten girls cos they all fancy him.

'And she's a terrible liar,' I went on. 'She thinks the whole world's against her and she's got to hurt them before they hurt her.'

'How do you know that?' says Nina, who's looking at me a bit strangely.

I couldn't tell her. It had just come to me. It was as much a surprise to me as it was to her.

'Well, I can think of at least half a dozen Year Ten girls like that,' said Omar. But then he frowned. 'I might have a school photo somewhere. It was taken at the end of last term. But it shows the whole of our year.'

He brought it down from upstairs. Year Nine, as it was then – over 200 of them – at the end of the summer term. We took it back to Nina's room and I studied it carefully, face by face. But she wasn't there.

'She might not have been there last term,' Nina said. 'She might have started this year.'

This was something to cling to, because I desperately wanted to believe that she was real. I think I knew, though, that she wasn't.

She was my doppelgänger and I was going to die.

We sat in gloomy silence for a while. Then Nina said: 'Well, looking on the bright side, three years is quite a long time. A lot can happen in three years.'

'Thanks, Nina,' I said.

'We might all be dead in a few years,' she says, 'according to my dad. Unless we all become eco-warriors like him.'

Nina's dad's an environmentalist. He works for the government, advising people on climate change and what to do about it. He's always buzzing with ideas. Mum says just talking to him makes her feel like going away and having a lie-down. His name's Tariq but Mum calls him Rabbit-on-a-Busy-Day, from *Winnie-the-Pooh*. I suppose it's because he doesn't think we've got much time left.

'Anyway, don't worry,' says Nina. 'It can't be worse than Waverley.'

It's all right for Nina. She believes in life after death. We've talked about it before. She believes that if you're a good Muslim you go to a place called Jannah, which is a kind of garden with lots of different levels, like terraces, according to how good you've been, and it's got all the things you longed for when you were on Earth.

But I've never really believed in anything like that. At best, I suppose I kind of hoped you might be reborn as someone else. Or some*thing* else. Like a bird or a wolf or a tree. Or if you were really lucky, the next Lionel Messi.

Now it looked like I was going to spend the whole of eternity with a ring in my nose looking like a dead sheep. Stuck at age fifteen for ever and ever. The worst age you can possibly be. Hating yourself and everybody else. The Ugly Duckling age, an inbetweener. Not exactly a child and not a grown-up.

OK, plenty of teenagers aren't like that, I know. Look at Omar. But the Spook was. She was the worst kind of inbetweener. That was what I was going to grow up into, and I was going to be stuck with it for the next billion years or so.

10

A Hundred Things to do Before You Die

What do you do if you've only got three years to live?

I guess you could think of a lot of things.

So could I. I even made a list.

Top of it was playing in the England Under-Fifteen Girls' Football Team.

But after that, in no particular order of preference:

- Climbing Gangkhar Puensum. (Gangkhar Puensum is in Bhutan on the border with China and is the highest unclimbed mountain in the world.)
- Swimming with great white sharks. (Don't

ask me why. I think because it seems more original than swimming with dolphins – *everybody* wants to do that – and it's certainly more dangerous. But if you've only got three years to live, why not? I thought I might leave it until the last day of the final year, though.)

- Sleeping in a haunted house. (An odd one, that, but I was beginning to have a thing about ghosts and I felt I needed to explore the subject a bit more thoroughly, before I became one.)

- Falling in love. (I know. I agonized over this because I wasn't sure I wanted to. On the other hand, I didn't want to die before I'd had at least one crack at it. Also, it would be nice to think of someone, apart from my parents and close friends, some *boy*, for instance, being gutted – no I don't mean gutted, I mean plunged into totally inconsolable grief – by my death, like Romeo in *Romeo and Juliet*, though I'm not sure I'd want him to kill himself; I'll have to think about that. Be nice to be kissed, too – properly kissed – but I guess that can be part of falling in love; it doesn't need to be a Thing to Do on its own.)

- And talking of my parents – bringing Mum and Dad together again. I wouldn't mind doing that before I die. I mean, really together, not just living in the same house, but so they love each other again. (Always assuming they did in the first place, which they must have because otherwise, what was the point of getting married or having me?)
- Sleeping in the open under the stars, and . . .
- Seeing the world from outer space. (Difficult to achieve, I know, but if I was going to leave the world I wanted to see it just once from the outside. And also, it might make me feel I could exist without being a part of it, if you know what I mean.)

I ran out of ideas after that, so I looked it up on my laptop – 100 things to do before you die. I couldn't believe some of the things I read.

Are you ready for this? This is what some people want to do:

1. Spend a whole day eating junk food without feeling guilty.
2. Brew your own beer.

3. Grow a beard and keep it on for at least a month.
4. Be a member of the audience in a TV show.
5. Be the boss.
6. Own one very expensive but absolutely wonderful business suit.
7. Spend Christmas on the beach drinking pina coladas.
8. Fart in a crowded space.
9. Lose more money than you can afford at roulette in Las Vegas.

And,

10. Be able to fill in your tax return.

How sad is that?

But that's not the worst. The worst, in my opinion, is this:

11. Reflect on your greatest weakness, and realize it is your greatest strength.

Aaagh!

Who are these people? And why do I hate them so

much? And why do I hate that last one in particular?

Reflect on your greatest weakness, and realize it is your greatest strength.

Well, one reason is that it's one of those crass sayings that sound so kind of . . . *wise* – but are so totally *mindless*.

I mean, it's like the kind of thing you might think of while you're drinking your Christmas pina coladas on the beach – when you've already had about eighty of them.

But let's give it a go. What is my greatest weakness? Difficult one. Lots of possibilities here. But let's go for Feelings of Almost Uncontrollable Rage – mostly directed against people whose ambition is to own one very expensive but absolutely wonderful business suit before they die.

I felt quite depressed.

I looked at my own list. Although it was, in my opinion, a much more imaginative and intelligent list than the Phantom Farter's, it had the same basic weakness.

It was all about *Me*.

Things *I* wanted to do for *Myself*.

It had nothing to do with doing things for other people.

Apart from wanting my parents to love each other, I suppose, and even then, that was really for me, too, in a way.

So that is why I began to think about what Nina had said about us all dying anyway unless we become eco-warriors.

The problem was, how was I going to make any difference?

I suppose I could do all the usual things like making sure the light switches aren't left on, and not leaving the tap running while I was cleaning my teeth and not eating so much food – and I promised myself I'd do all of that and more – but it wasn't exactly . . . *uplifting*. It wasn't exactly the stuff of eco-warriors.

I wanted to do something that would make a real difference, a dramatic difference. Like sailing a dinghy in front of a whaling fleet to save the whales.

I know that's all about me, too, but given that I was going to die, I needed to feel some sense of achievement. A sense that I'd made a difference during my short lifetime, or at least tried to, like the people who run marathons for charity when they're suffering from some incurable disease.

I thought about this through most of Sunday but nothing fantastic came to mind. I was still thinking about it in school on Monday.

The last lesson of the afternoon was history. Mr Mooney. Loony Mooney, we call him, mainly because he gets all worked up about things that happened hundreds of years ago. His favourite expression is 'Isn't that amazing???!!!!' And he stares at you all goggle-eyed with his arms spread out, like he's *Amazed!*

We were doing the Middle Ages, which I think I've already mentioned, and Loony was talking about the Crusades. Most of it went in one ear and out the other. I mean, there were times I was interested in the Middle Ages and times when I wasn't, and this was one of the times when I wasn't.

But then suddenly he says something that makes me switch on.

'Then one day, in the year 1212, a twelve-year-old shepherd boy from France called Etienne, or Stephen in English, had an amazing idea . . .'

I think it was the two things really. The fact that this kid was twelve, about the same age as me, and the fact that he had an amazing idea, when that was just what I was trying to come up with.

So I started to pay more attention.

The amazing idea turned out to be a disappointment

– at least from my point of view. Stephen's amazing idea was to lead a Crusade to the Holy Land.

Now, I don't know how much you know about the Crusades and normally I'd be the last person to tell you about them, despite my interest in history, because to be perfectly honest the Crusades is not my favourite part of it.

The word 'crusade' is used for all sorts of things nowadays. You can have a crusade against litter, you can have a crusade against serving Turkey Twizzlers for school dinners. But in the Middle Ages, a Crusade meant only one thing: a load of Christian knights and soldiers marching on Jerusalem.

The reason they were so keen on Jerusalem was because it was the city of King David, the King of the Jews in the Bible, and Christ had lived and died there. So it was a holy city to millions of Christians and Jews. But it was holy to Muslims, too, and so for hundreds of years they all fought wars over it.

This seemed ridiculous to me but I suppose it would have made more sense if I'd been listening properly.

Anyway, lots of Crusades were sent there and they were all a failure – at least from the Christian point of view. So this is where Stephen the shepherd boy comes in. He said he had been called on by Christ himself to lead a Children's Crusade, and that the children would succeed where the grown-ups had failed.

The first thing he did was to go to the King of France and ask for his support. But the king told him to go home. So then he went around the country preaching, which was what you did before Facebook, calling on all the children in France to follow him and march on Jerusalem. They would have to cross the Mediterranean Sea but Stephen said God had promised to part the waves for them so they would be able to walk all the way there.

Amazingly, according to Loony, over 30,000 children came from all over France and Germany. All under the age of twelve.

Many of the children's parents came after them and tried to drag them back home, but the Crusade was supported by a lot of priests who thought that the children would shame the rulers of Europe into doing something themselves.

So this vast army of kids sets off on the long march to the Holy Land. And some of the priests go with them. There's hardly any food or water and lots of them die on the way through France. But eventually those that are left reach the sea and wait for the waves to part, as Stephen had said they would.

But the waves didn't part.

At which point, most of the kids pack up and go home. The rest camp out on the beach and wait for the miracle to happen.

But instead, these two merchants turn up and they say they'll take them in their ships.

The names of these merchants were Hugh the Iron and William the Pig. I mean! But Stephen says OK. So all the kids climb aboard and the ships set sail for Jerusalem.

And that's the last anyone hears of them. For eighteen years, anyway. Then this man comes back from Egypt with a curious tale.

He says he was one of the young priests who marched south with the children and sailed with them to Jerusalem. He said that as soon as the ships were out of sight of land they were surrounded by Muslim pirates who took the children prisoner and sold them as slaves in Egypt. And the whole thing was arranged by Hugh the Iron and William the Pig.

Big surprise.

And so that was the end of the Children's Crusade.

All that came out of it, said Loony, was a fairy tale

– or a folk tale, I suppose you'd call it – the story of the Pied Piper of Hamelin. If you don't know it, look it up because it's worth reading in full, but basically it's about a town in Germany that was overrun by rats. The town council tried everything they could to get rid of them, but nothing worked. Then this funny little man turned up. He was dressed in clothes of many colours, which they called 'pied' in those days, and he played a pipe, a bit like a flute or a recorder. So they called him the Pied Piper. Anyway, he said he could get rid of the rats if the council gave him a bag of gold, and the councillors were so desperate they agreed. So the Pied Piper played this strange music which made all the rats come out of the sewers and follow him. They followed him out of the town and all the way to the coast and then they ran into the sea and were drowned.

But when the Pied Piper came back to Hamelin and asked for his bag of gold, the councillors tried to get out of the deal. They said it was ridiculous for him to say it was his music that made the rats leave and that they probably would have left anyway. So the Pied Piper started to play his pipe again – and this time it wasn't the rats who followed him. It was the children. Every child in Hamelin under the age of twelve. And the only one who came back was a little lame boy who couldn't keep up. The rest were never seen again.

'Isn't that amazing?' says Loony Mooney.

'Why?' I said.

Everyone turned to look at me.

'Because it's the same story as the Children's Crusade,' says Loony. 'More or less.'

'Except for the rats,' I pointed out. 'And the piper.'

'Oh well, if you're going to be picky,' says Loony. And then the bell went for the end of the lesson.

Even so, he'd given me something to think about. It wasn't the fact that all those kids had set off to march to the Holy Land. It was the bit about them shaming the grown-ups into doing something.

I was still thinking about this when I was cycling back home across the Common.

It was one of those fantastic days in autumn when the sky is a hard, clear blue and the trees are all red and orange and gold. I was cycling down the path with trees on either side and the leaves were drifting down in front of me, and I felt like I was in some kind of fairy tale myself.

I know that sounds corny and it's not the way I usually feel on my way home from school – usually

I'm too busy looking out for the parks police. But I was in a strange kind of mood. I was part happy because it was so good to be alive and the world seemed such a lovely place, and I was part sad because it all seemed to be coming to an end. I guess that's a typical autumn feeling. No matter how lovely it is you know the leaves will keep falling and the nights will keep drawing in and then the first storms of November will strip the trees bare and it will be winter. And it was particularly bad for me this year because I was pretty sure now that the Spook *was* an omen and I was only going to see a couple more autumns and then I'd be dead.

Then I saw this bulldozer. Or it might have been a JCB. It was only a small one and it wasn't doing any harm. It wasn't actually doing anything, in fact — it was just parked there, like it was finished for the day. It looked like it was being used to dig a ditch by the side of the path, cos there were all these big black plastic pipes lying around, probably for drainage or sewage or something. But it had torn up all the earth and uprooted a load of shrubs and small trees and it just looked such a mess.

And I really hated it.

It seemed to me that the more beautiful the world

was, the more likely it was that someone, usually with a bulldozer, would come along and destroy it. Gouging out huge chunks of earth and uprooting the trees and smashing and burning everything in sight.

I knew this was ridiculous – in this particular case, anyway. Ridiculous and childish. And that once the pipes were laid, the same bulldozer would push all the earth back in the ditch and flatten it all out and that by next summer the grass would have grown back over it and you'd never know it had been torn up in the first place. They're very useful things, bulldozers – and JCBs – I know all that. We've got to have drains, we've got to have roads, we've got to have airports and shops and houses, I know. They're probably quite good for digging graves, too.

But even so, the way I was feeling at this particular moment, that little bulldozer seemed to me like a symbol of all the things that were making the world an uglier and more dangerous place. Destroying the rainforests, polluting the rivers and the seas, wiping out entire species – that little bulldozer had a lot to answer for.

I remember a set of pictures Dad showed me once. They were nothing to do with war or natural disaster and I'm not sure he ever did anything with them, apart from show them to me. They were of a load of old bulldozers and JCBs and tractors and dumper trucks in a field – I think it was in France. There were dozens of them. It looked like they'd made their way here from all over the country to die, the way elephants do in Africa. A graveyard for metal monsters.

I expect someone meant to use them for scrap metal but then forgot, and they'd just been left to rust and rot away. The grass and the trees were growing up all around them and even through them. Brambles and dog roses and various other things I didn't know the names of had grown right over the top of the cabs, and small trees were growing up through their innards and kind of exploding out of the top of them.

Dad called it the Revenge of the Earth on the Earthmovers.

I knew I was part of the problem. That it was mainly because of me and millions of people like me that we needed the earthmovers. But we also needed the Earth and we were killing it.

And that's when I had my big idea.

11

The Zeitgeist

'A children's crusade?'

'Well . . .'

'To save the world?'

This is Nina when I tell her. She's looking at me like I've completely lost it. But I've been getting this from Nina since I was about two; I try not to let it get to me.

'Not the world,' I said. 'The Earth.'

'There's a difference, is there?'

There *was* a difference. At least in my own mind. But it was difficult to put into words. The world is kind of – *hard*. Hard word, hard place. Busy, busy. Full of itself. Full of busy people doing busy things. You hear about the world of business, the world of finance, the world of fashion, the world of politics . . . I'm not into saving *them*. I'm not saying they don't need to be saved but . . . The Earth is something else. Softer, gentler, *homelier*. It's a softer sound too, when you say it aloud. The Earth. It kind of breathes. Like breath itself, or the hearth. The place that gives you life, warmth, security. The Earth is our home, our nest, and we're destroying it.

I didn't say this to Nina because I couldn't put it into words at the time, but even if I had, I think she'd have still given me her look. It might even have been worse.

'So how are you going to save . . . *the Earth*?' she says. Breathily.

'Not me,' I said. '*Us.*'

Nina is a very practical person. I'm not. Generally speaking. Everyone says I'm a bit too much of a dreamer, except when I'm playing football. But I'd been thinking carefully about this and I had some very practical ideas.

'We're going to have a conference,' I said. 'A children's conference. On the environment. We're going to hire a big hall – a conference hall – and we're going to invite hundreds of children our age from all over the world to come and talk about what's happening to the environment where they live, and say what they think should be done about it.'

'Wow,' said Nina.

Nina often says 'Wow', but it doesn't mean 'Wow, that's amazing!' Not when she says it in that tone of voice, with her eyes sliding from side to side like she's just run into someone who's escaped from a prison for the criminally insane, and she's looking to see if there's any help around, or if there's any more of them creeping up on her.

'And how are they going to get here?' she says. 'Walk? Like the Children's Crusade? You going to part the waves like Simon What's-his-face?'

Very funny. I don't know about being a lawyer; she should think about going into stand-up. I think of saying this but I don't. I want Nina on my side.

'Stephen,' I said.

'What?' she said.

'His name was Stephen. Not Simon. Stephen the shepherd boy. No. They're not going to walk. They're going to fly here.'

I was sounding very confident about this, I know, but you have to with Nina or she'll tear you to pieces.

'Fly?' she says, as if this is the most ridiculous thing she's ever heard of, like they'd have to sprout wings.

134

'Yes. You know, in planes.'

That shuts her up for a moment, but only a moment. 'So who's going to pay for it?' she says.

'The airlines. They're going to fly them for free, to show how much they care for the environment. And we're going to get lots of sponsors to pay for the conference hall and the hotels and everything else.'

'Wow,' she says again.

Now I've known Nina all my life, and this is a different kind of 'Wow'. It's half mocking and it's half impressed. It's half – 'Wow, I knew you were mental but I didn't think you were *that* mental', and it's half – 'Wow, I wish *I'd* thought of that.'

'We're going to come up with a plan of action,' I said. 'A series of concrete proposals. And we're going to send them to the United Nations.'

'Now you're scaring me,' she says. 'Where did you get all this stuff?'

I shrugged modestly. In fact I'd got the concrete proposals bit from something I'd heard on the news, but most of it was me.

'You're serious about this?'

'Totally.'

'OK, if you make it happen – big if – what d'you think's going to come out of it? I mean, a load of kids. Who's going to listen? They can't actually *do* anything.'

'Maybe not,' I said, 'but they can shame the people who *can* do something. You know – like the Children's Crusade.'

She just looked at me.

'Remember? Loony Mooney and the Children's Crusade? That's why the Pope supported them,' I reminded her. 'He thought it would shame all the grown-ups – the kings and the princes and the knights and all that – into getting off their bums and doing something.'

'So, you going to talk to the Pope?' she says.

'No,' I said. 'I'm going to talk to your dad.'

That wiped the smirk off her face.

So we march downstairs to see her dad.

Now I'd better tell you about her dad and me, even though it's a bit embarrassing.

He's very big, Nina's dad, about six foot four and he's got this big black beard – well, it used to be black; it's more grey now. He'd like to dye it but Nina says her mum won't let him. He's very kind and sweet and all that, but he doesn't look it. He looks quite fierce. And he shouts a lot.

'Dad's off on a rant,' Nina says.

I was terrified of him when I was little. I used to hide under the table. And when she first told me he was an environmentalist, I didn't know what it meant. I thought she meant he was a *mentalist*.

Round our way if you call someone a mentalist you mean they're mad. I found out later that it also means someone with supernatural powers, like a mind-reader. But that's much the same, really.

So Nina, of course, she tells him. 'Kit thinks you're a mentalist.' So whenever he caught me looking at him, he'd stop whatever he was doing and kind of stalk around me, muttering to himself. We were like two cats waiting for the first one to make a move. Then he'd suddenly fling his arms about as if he was being attacked by a swarm of bees, or he'd pretend to find an insect in his hair and eat it.

So although he doesn't do that any more, and I've well got over being scared of him, I'm still a bit, not exactly nervous with him, but cautious. Just in case he goes off on one.

So we march into the kitchen where he's sitting reading the paper and Nina says: 'Kit wants to talk to you.'

'Oh yes?' he says, putting the paper down.

'She's got an idea,' she says. 'She wants to explain

it to you. Go on,' she says to me. 'Explain it.'

So I did. And he was great.

'I'm very impressed,' he said. I looked at Nina. I nearly stuck my tongue out but I was trying to be grown-up. He looked at me curiously. 'What made you think of it?'

I thought I'd better not mention the Spook, but I told him about the Children's Crusade.

'I don't know much about that,' he says. 'What happened to them?'

'They all died,' says Nina.

'That was because it was badly organized,' I said. 'Besides, we're not going to march on Jerusalem. And we're not going to fight anyone. We're just going to get people's attention. And tell them we don't want them to leave us a – you know – a wasteland to live in. We want to shame people into doing something about it before it's too late.'

He's looking at me in amazement.

'Right on,' he said. 'Good for you. And you can stop looking so superior, madam –' This is to Nina – 'It's a brilliant idea.'

Then he started being practical. How were we going to publicize this conference? How were we going to find our delegates? I'd vaguely thought of using the Internet but he had better ideas. Names of people and organizations we needed to contact. He said he'd put a couple of his interns on it, to draft the emails for us.

'The main thing is to get one of the airlines on board,' he said. 'And find some rich sponsors.'

I was starting to get nervous. Until now it had just been an idea – and a vague idea at that. Tariq was talking about it as if it could really happen.

And then Nina sticks her oar in.

This is typical of Nina. Ever since we were kids we've had this thing – I come up with an idea and she rubbishes it. I must be mad, she says. And then gradually she comes around to thinking it's not such a bad idea after all. And then she starts to take it over and before I know where I am it's *her* idea, and we're doing it *her* way – and then it's *totally* mad.

I'll give you one example. When we were about seven or eight, I had this idea for Halloween. Instead of dressing up as witches, like we usually did, and knocking on doors for Trick or Treat, we should have a collection *in aid* of witches. We should make people realize how awful it was when witches were hanged or burned at the stake. I said we should wheel a dummy witch round in a cart from house to house and say she was going to be burned on Tooting Bec unless they donated ten pence to stop it.

But I didn't mean we should have a *real* witch. And I certainly didn't mean we should have a *real* bonfire. Not on Tooting Bec. The parks police would go mental.

Then Nina takes over. Until then she's been going on about how stupid it is, and how no one's going to give us anything. Next thing I know she's persuaded Sapphire Enron to dress up in rags and sit in a wheelbarrow with her cat – Pusskin – while we push them from door to door. But instead of asking for ten pence to *save* her from being burned, we charge people twenty pence for them to come and watch.

It was horrible. We raised over ten pounds. And we're pushing Sapphire and her cat to the Common with this huge crowd of kids behind us going '*Burn the witch, burn the witch, burn the witch . . .*'

Nina said she hadn't actually planned it. Not like this. But she said that when we reached the Common she didn't know what to do next. It seemed a bit lame to just say, 'Well, that's it, people. Come back next Halloween.' And besides, she'd have had to give them back their money.

So before I could think of a better idea, she's got

everyone running around the Common looking for sticks to build a bonfire.

She said later it was all pretend – of course she wasn't going to set fire to anyone – and anyway, she didn't think they'd find enough sticks. But she looked pretty convincing at the time, wearing her brother's hoodie and waving this torch around like the Wailing Monk of Bec. It convinced Sapphire Enron, anyway. You should have heard the noise she made. And as for Pusskin – I don't think I've ever seen a cat move so fast.

Then the parks police arrived.

We were in so much trouble, I can't tell you. There's kids running off in all directions and the five of us – the five witch-burners – standing in a huddle with our heads down and the police all around us and Sapphire Enron with blood pouring down her arm where Pusskin scratched her, wailing that we'd tried to kill her.

We were all a bit tearful. Except Nina, of course. I thought I saw her bottom lip trembling but it was only with the effort of trying to find the right words to explain herself. She wasn't so good with words in those days; she was only eight. The best she could come up with was 'we were only playing'.

Children shouldn't play with fire, the police said, or they get burned.

Then they piled us in the police car. I thought they were going to lock us up but they just took us back to our parents and told them what we'd been up to. There was hell to pay, of course. I was with Nina when they handed her over to Tariq and Shella. For once she didn't say a word. She just stood there biting her lip while Tariq ranted and raved at her.

Years later, though, when the matter was brought up again in the middle of one of their epic arguments – they can go on for hours – I heard her tell him she was trying to demonstrate that what he called 'civilized society' was just a thin veneer over barbarism, and that if you removed all restraints people would revert to savagery in no time, especially kids. I think she'd just been reading *Lord of the Flies*.

I'm probably giving the wrong impression about Nina. People say she's too clever by half, or too advanced for her years, but she's really a very good person. Everyone says she's got strong moral convictions. But having strong moral convictions doesn't mean you're always right. Look at Stephen the shepherd boy.

So I know exactly what happens when Nina takes

over something. The witch-burning on Tooting Bec wasn't a one-off. I can't tell you how many times I've nearly ended up in jail because of her.

And now she's doing it again.

'We need a celebrity,' she says.

I knew then that she was up for it. She'd decided it wasn't such a mad idea after all. And amazingly, I was pleased.

Pleased.

'Like who?' I said.

'Well, like Miley Cyrus or Robert Pattinson or Megan Fox . . .'

She could see we weren't that impressed, especially not her dad, who's never heard of any of them.

'Or people who get involved in lost causes,' she said. 'I mean *good* causes,' she added hastily. 'Like Matt Damon or Justin Bieber or Lady Gaga – or – or Posh and Becks,' she says, desperately trying to think of someone her dad's heard of.

'OK,' says Tariq. 'But it should be someone with a real interest in the environment.'

Nina glares at him like she does when she thinks he's trying to be difficult. But then her face clears and she says: 'Leo Lyall!'

'What?' says Tariq.

'Not what, who,' says Nina, rolling her eyes. 'He's a rock star, Dad. Leo Lyall and the Zeitgeist.'

'The Zeitgeist?'

'That's his band. It means the spirit of the times.'

'Thank you, Nina,' he says. 'I do know what *zeitgeist* means.'

I can't say I did. I found out later it was a German word. *Zeit* for times and *geist* for ghost or spirit. Maybe this was Nina's idea of a joke – against me. I should have taken it as a warning.

'They do a lot of stuff for the environment,' Nina was saying. 'I've read about it. Their last concert was for the rainforest and they raised millions.'

'Sounds good to me,' says Tariq. 'What about you, Kit?'

And I shrugged.

I can't believe it now.

I shrugged?

If I'd had the faintest idea where it was going to lead us, I'd have made more noise than Sapphire Enron in the wheelbarrow. I'd have been out of there faster than her cat Pusskin. I'd have stopped trying to save the planet and gone in for something a lot safer, like climbing Gangkhar Puensum, or swimming with great white sharks.

'So let's rock and roll,' says Tariq.

And we both rolled our eyes.

12

Fort Doom

So here we are at Battersea Heliport waiting for the Zeitgeist.

I think it was only then, as I watched it coming up the river towards me, that it hit me. If Nina hadn't been clutching my arm so tightly I think I might have made a dash for the nearest exit and jumped on the first bus back to Balham.

The Zeitgeist, I should tell you, as well as being the spirit of the times and the name of Leo Lyall's rock band, was also the name of his helicopter. His *private* helicopter. He'd sent it to pick us up and whisk us back to his pad at the mouth of the Thames. His London pad, that is. Apparently he also has pads in New York, California and the Caribbean. I was a bit sorry we weren't going to one of them instead, but only a bit. I felt completely out of my depth already.

From the way Nina was hanging on to me, I wondered if she was, too. But then I saw her eyes and they were shining with excitement. Excitement and a sort of triumph. A bit like they'd been when we were pushing the wheelbarrow towards Tooting Bec with Sapphire Enron in it and her cat, and half the kids in the neighbourhood behind us going, 'Burn the witch!'

There were only four of us this time. Me, Nina, Tariq and a woman called Ella who worked in his office – I think she was a press officer or a publicist or something. Tariq was trying to look cool, but I could tell from the way he kept frowning and scratching his beard that he was almost as nervous as we were. He'd been knocked out by how fast Leo Lyall had got back to us. We'd only sent the email a week ago. And that was to his website. None of us, not even Nina, had any real hope that it would ever get through to him. Now he was sending his private helicopter to pick us up.

'Isn't this fantastic?' Ella had said to me when she met us at the heliport. 'Get Leo Lyall aboard and we're laughing.'

I didn't feel like laughing. Leo Lyall was huge. When people said the Zeitgeist they didn't just mean his band, they meant *him* – like *he* was the spirit of the times. He was not only famous as a rock star; he was famous as a campaigner. He had thrown himself into campaigns all over the world, mostly to do with saving the environment. He didn't just raise money, he led marches and protests, he joined sit-ins, he'd even joined in battles against the police and the army. He said he was on the side of the small people against big business and big government.

Well, we were small people, all right. And I was feeling smaller by the minute.

The moment the helicopter landed, a woman in a brown leather flying jacket jumped out and ran towards us, ducking under the blast from the rotor blades.

'I'm May,' she says. Or it might have been Mei, because she looked Chinese. 'I'm Leo's PA,' she said. She spoke with a slight American accent. 'Which one's Kit?'

The first thing she asks. *Which one's Kit?* As if I'm famous or something. I'm stunned. I can't speak. Why is she picking *me* out?

'This is Kit,' says Tariq, putting his hand on my

shoulder. I was glad to feel it there. He might be a pain at times, Tariq, but he's very solid.

May or Mei gives me this sharp, piercing look and sticks out her hand. She was incredibly beautiful; she looked like something out of a fashion shoot or a movie. A film star playing a Chinese fighter pilot. I could see Nina taking in the leather jacket and the torn jeans and the boots and I reckoned I knew what her next look would be, if she could talk Shella into paying for it.

Mei shook everyone else's hand, too, but she obviously didn't want to hang about. She led us back to the Zeitgeist in a stooping, ducking run, and as soon as we were strapped in, it took off again.

We headed straight down the middle of the river. It was another clear autumn day and you could see right across the city. We had cans on so we could hear instructions from the pilot, but Mei was doing most of the talking, giving us a running commentary. I'd never been in a helicopter before and to be honest I felt a bit sick – more from the thought of what I'd got myself into than anything to do with the ride. It was smoother than being in a car. In *our* car anyway. Apart from the noise and the fact that we were doing about a hundred miles an hour it was like we were floating in a giant bubble through the heart of London.

Gradually I began to pay more attention. We were flying right over Westminster now, with the Houses of Parliament on one side and the London Eye on the other and the whole city spread out beneath us with the river twisting and turning through the middle of it. Mei's still doing her commentary, pointing out the famous landmarks like the Shard and the Gherkin and Buckingham Palace and Saint Paul's Cathedral, and we're looking this way and that like spectators at a tennis match who can't actually see the ball cos it's moving too fast; before you can catch up with it, it's moved on. One minute we're over Tower Bridge and the Tower of London, then it's the Isle of Dogs with the red light on top of Canary Wharf winking away at us, and then we're over Greenwich and the Thames Barrier . . .

Then we left the city far behind us and headed out over the estuary.

Even though I've lived in London all my life, I didn't know much about the Thames Estuary. All I knew was it used to be where millions of Londoners went for their summer holidays before they started going to places like Spain and Greece and Turkey. In those days it was Southend-on-Sea and Herne Bay and Whitstable. I'd seen pictures of them – old black and white photographs at an exhibition we went to with the school. Promenades and Punch and Judy shows, whelks and jellied eels, sandy beaches and funfairs and millions of people having fun for the two weeks in the year they were officially allowed to: paddling in the water or playing ball games on the crowded beaches or just sitting on deckchairs in the sun with the women handing out egg sandwiches and the men with their trousers rolled up to their knees wearing handkerchiefs on their heads and reading newspapers.

It didn't look like that now. Instead of the helter-skelters and the rollercoasters there were oil refineries and power stations, and instead of thousands of people paddling at the edge of the water and waving up at us there were hundreds and hundreds of wind turbines.

And then we were heading out into the open sea. At least it seemed like it – a vast expanse of open water with a few ships, like fat slugs with long silver trails stretching out behind them.

Then suddenly, without any warning, we slide sideways and start to go down. For one awful moment I thought something had gone wrong with the engine and we were going to crash. I could see nothing solid to land on, nothing obvious anyway, not even a sandbank. Then I saw these strange shapes standing out of the water. At first I thought they were more wind turbines, but they were more like giant insects or battle machines from some fantasy war-game, with big round bodies on long spindly legs. We were practically skimming the surface towards them now, and the closer we came, the weirder they looked.

There were six or seven of them standing in a huddle and it seemed like they were watching us with hundreds of cold, staring eyes. Then I saw that the bodies were buildings and the eyes were windows with the sunlight glinting on them. But what were they doing out in the middle of the Thames Estuary?

'Welcome to Fort Doom,' I heard Mei's voice in my earphones.

'Wow,' I heard Nina say. And for once it was a proper 'Wow'. When they'd said Leo had a pad out in the Thames Estuary, I thought they meant somewhere *beside* the estuary. I didn't realize they actually meant *in* it.

Fort Doom dated from the Second World War, Mei told us, and it was one of a series of forts armed with anti-aircraft guns and strung out across the estuary to stop German planes flying upriver to bomb London. But after the war they'd been abandoned and left to rot, until about five years ago when Leo had decided one of them would make a nice place to live.

By now the helicopter was hovering directly above one of the towers and we could see there was a landing pad marked out on the roof. We settled on it so gently you could hardly feel the bump.

We all piled out and Mei hurried us into a little shed with steps leading down into what she called the reception area. It was like an old-fashioned hotel lobby with lots of sofas and armchairs and potted palms and a grand piano. So far, so ordinary (except, of course, that it was in a disused World War Two fort in the middle of the Thames Estuary). But what was not so ordinary was that the piano was playing. By itself. You could see the keys moving up and down and you could hear the music, but there was no pianist. It was as if a ghost was playing it. And what made it even more ghostly was that it was playing to an empty room. Then I heard a small cry from Nina, like a cut-off scream, and I turned round and saw the dancers.

There were six of them – three couples – dancing round a small ballroom at the back of the room, behind the potted palms. The men wore black evening suits and bow ties and the women wore old-fashioned ball gowns. But they weren't *real* men and women. They looked like the dummies you see in shop windows. They all had fixed smiles on their faces and they were moving very stiffly in a circle round the dance floor. It was like a kind of giant music box.

'It's a mechanical tea dance,' said Mei when she saw what we were looking at. 'It was made for the Emperor Mobutu when he ruled the Congo. Leo bought it at an auction. He's into oddities.'

Then we heard a noise, like a helicopter taking off. It *was* a helicopter taking off. *Our* helicopter. We saw it out of the window beetling away over the water.

'Don't worry, they're coming back,' Mei said when she saw the expressions on our faces. 'They've just gone to pick something up. Let me give you the guided tour.'

The seven towers were linked by metal catwalks over the water and we followed Mei from one to the other, getting more and more freaked out by Leo's 'oddities'.

The first place she took us was the recording studio. This was more or less what you might expect

– 'state of the art', said Mei – except that half the floor was made of glass and you could see the Thames swirling around beneath your feet. Mei said if you played a wrong note or if Leo got bored, the glass slid back and you were dumped in it. Everyone laughed but she didn't look as if she was joking.

This was where the band had recorded their latest album, 'Requiem for a Dying Planet,' she said. You probably know it. It's been top of the world downloads for years. All the tracks are about the environment and the mess it's in. The title song is a combination of music and sound effects, like birds singing in the rainforest, or a lion roaring, or whales doing their thing, and the sounds of chainsaws and bulldozers and trees crashing to the ground and being burned. And from time to time you hear Leo's voice, not really singing but just repeating single words or lines in lots of different languages. It goes on for about a quarter of an hour. Very Zeitgeist.

The next tower was the gym. This was 'state of the art', too. The only thing that made it any different from any other gym in the world was that instead of the usual mirrors, the walls were painted with scenes from Hell. The most vivid scenes you can imagine. In fact I hope you can't imagine them.

Some of them were disgusting.

'It encourages Leo to lose those extra pounds,' Mei explained.

'You don't go to Hell because you're fat,' said Nina primly.

'Try telling Leo that,' said Mei, but she could see we thought it was pretty gross, and Tariq was scowling and tugging his beard so she whisked us out of there.

'There's a swimming pool on the floor below,' she said, 'but there's nothing particularly interesting about it.'

I thought there almost certainly was, but I wasn't saying anything. We were on our way to the next tower when we heard the sound of the helicopter again, and I saw it in the distance heading back towards us.

The next tower was a cinema. A really old-fashioned cinema. Apparently it was an exact replica of the Margate Astoria, which was built in the 1920s, but had been bombed by the German Air Force.

'Leo saw some pictures of what it looked like inside and decided he wanted one just like it,' said Mei.

'Art Deco, isn't it?' said Nina, gazing up at the ceiling.

'It is.' Mei looked surprised. 'I'm impressed. Do you like Art Deco?'

'Some of it,' says Nina airily. 'Is that what Leo's into?'

I closed my eyes and made a wish, but when I opened them she was still there.

'Apparently it reminded him of a cinema in Tooting where he watched movies as a child,' said Mei, 'until they turned it into a bingo hall.'

'In Tooting?' I looked at her sharply.

'Yes. Leo was brought up there,' she said. 'Kind of cute, don't you think? Tooting. When I first heard it I called it Too-ting, like a town in China.'

I wondered if Nina knew that Leo Lyall had been brought up in Tooting, but she was still gazing around at all the stuff on the walls and I couldn't catch her eye.

'Why did the German Air Force bomb the Astoria cinema in Margate?' Tariq asks suddenly, as if it's been preying on his mind.

Mei shrugged. 'I really have no idea,' she said. 'Maybe they were aiming at something else and missed?'

'Or maybe they were showing a film the Germans didn't like,' said Nina.

Mei smiled at her. I could see Nina had made a hit. 'Leo sometimes invites parties of senior citizens from Margate to come and watch a movie here,' Mei said, 'to remind them of when they were younger.'

'That's very nice of him,' said Ella.

'And then he bombs them,' said Nina under her breath, so only I could hear her.

'But mostly he just sits here and watches movies by himself.' Mei was still talking. 'And I have to dress up as an old-fashioned usherette and serve him ice-cream.'

If this was another joke, she was very good at doing deadpan.

The next tower had been turned into a conservatory. The roof had been taken off and replaced with glass and the whole place filled with plants – amazing plants, even whole trees, all hung about with creepers and stuff, so that it was just like walking into a rainforest. And then Nina grabbed my arm and pointed and I looked up and saw hundreds and hundreds of butterflies flying about and feeding on the flowers at the very tops of the trees. It was the most fantastic thing I'd ever seen, even in this place. And it was so quiet. Quieter even than the real rainforest, I imagine, because there was no sound of birds or monkeys or any other living thing. The only sound was the soft hiss of the steam pipes that kept the plants moist – that and the steady drip, drip of water.

'No parrots?' said Ella, looking up at the trees.

'Absolutely not,' said Mei. 'Leo won't have any captive birds or animals of any kind.' I was about to remind her about the butterflies, but I suppose as they're insects, technically speaking, they don't count. 'Only the snakes,' she added. 'He doesn't seem to mind the snakes being captive. But he insists they keep to a vegetarian diet.'

Nina caught my eye and tapped her head with her finger.

'Bats,' she said. I didn't know if she meant Mei or Leo Lyall. Probably both of them.

'Oh yes, he also permits bats,' said Mei, who must have been able to hear like one, 'but he keeps them in his bedroom.'

We didn't get to see Leo's bedroom, which was probably just as well. After she'd shown us the conservatory, Mei led us back to the reception area and we sat around twiddling our thumbs while the ghost pianist played a waltz and the dancers danced on. I could tell Tariq was getting restless.

'So when do we get to meet the star of the show?' he said to Mei after a few minutes.

'Soon, I hope,' said Mei, with a smile like one of the dancers.

'But he is here?' said Tariq, not smiling at all, probably because it had just dawned on him that Leo wasn't here and would probably never be here, not while we were.

'Not yet,' said Mei. She looked at her phone. 'He must be running late.'

'I see,' said Tariq in this steely voice he has when he thinks he's been mucked about. 'So who is here, apart from us? And them.' He nodded his head towards the dancers.

'Only Hal,' she said, still smiling.

'Hal?' frowned Tariq, looking round for him. 'Who's Hal when he's at home?'

'Hal is the computer who runs all of this. That is what Leo calls him. After the computer in *2001*.'

I didn't have the slightest idea what she was talking about but Tariq seemed to.

'You mean the Stanley Kubrick movie?'

'Correct. Leo has watched it many times.'

'The computer that went mad,' said Tariq, 'and tried to murder the crew?'

I rolled my eyes at Nina.

'Correct,' said Mei again. 'But our Hal is much nicer than that. He feeds the snakes and the bats, makes sure there are no intruders, keeps everything in good order. All sorts of things. I don't know what we would do without him.'

'So – the cameras and everything . . . ?' Tariq looked up at the one that was watching us from behind the reception desk. I could tell he wasn't convinced.

'They are for Hal. So he can see what's going on.'

'And if he doesn't like what he sees?'

'Ah, well usually Hal can handle it, but if he thinks he can't, he sends for back-up from the shore. They can be here in minutes.'

Then suddenly she stood up and crossed to one of the windows. We crowded round and looked out. There was a speedboat cutting through the water towards us from the direction of London. I wondered if Hal had called for back-up. But no, it wasn't the police or the SAS.

'Here he is at last,' said Mei.

It was Leo.

13

Leo's Den

It was going so fast. All I could see was a dark figure hunched over the wheel, almost lost in a cloud of spray. Then the boat slowed down for the final approach and he stood up. He was wearing a long black raincoat and shades, his long hair streaming behind him in the wind. I swear I could hear a blast of rock music, but it might have been in my mind.

'Leo always likes to make an entrance,' Mei said.

The boat disappeared under the tower and we lost sight of it for a minute, but then various lights started to flash on and off, and there was a loud beeping noise like a van makes when it's reversing.

'Better move back,' said Mei. We already were,

we didn't need her to tell us. A large crack had opened in the floor.

The crack widened and we could see water swirling below and the speedboat bobbing about next to one of the piers. Then he came clambering up the ladder towards us. Leo Lyall in person.

At least he didn't just appear in a puff of red smoke, like a demon in a pantomime, but it was pretty close. There's a song Mum plays sometimes, a real oldie, even for her. It goes, 'You walked into the party, like you were walking onto a yacht . . .' Well, that's Leo Lyall when he stepped off the ladder and walked into the lobby of Fort Doom.

I'd read quite a bit about him since we heard he wanted to meet us, and I knew he was a bit weird. Well, more than a bit. I suppose it's what you expect from a rock star, but even so, some of the things he'd done . . . I don't just mean the usual things of wrecking hotel rooms and taking drugs and beating up photographers. That was just average crazy.

Leo Lyall was totally insane.

One of the things he'd done, just as an example, was buy an old Russian submarine, arm it with torpedoes, and set off to sink the Japanese whaling fleet. He didn't get very far because the submarine broke down and had to be towed back to harbour, but it shows what he was like. Nina said it was only a publicity stunt, but still . . . I was surprised they hadn't locked him up years ago. It turned out they had, lots of times, but they kept on letting him out. Nina said he had very good lawyers.

Mei went to meet him and he bent to kiss her. On the lips, I noticed. I wondered if she was his girlfriend, or if this was the way he greeted all the women who worked for him. Then she led him over to introduce us.

I'd seen him before, of course, plenty of times, on television, but he looked different in real life. On TV, when he's performing, or even when he's being interviewed, he looks totally out of it. I wouldn't say he looked *normal* in real life, but at least he looked like he was a member of the human race.

He had reddish-blond hair and a beard – not much of one but more than designer stubble – and his face was quite tanned but not too much. He'd taken off his shades and his eyes were this really deep shade of blue, almost violet. I felt him looking at me the way Mei had at the heliport, kind of piercing and questioning at the same time. I felt embarrassed. Even though the conference had been my idea originally, the email we'd sent had both our names on it – mine and Nina's – and I couldn't think of any reason why it was me they seemed to be interested in, more than her. It isn't usually the case, believe me.

I wondered if they knew something about me, like I was a great footballer or something – which just shows how ridiculous I am. He didn't talk much, though. In fact he seemed a bit tongue-tied, even shy. He had this slight American accent, I suppose because he spent so much time in the US. He certainly didn't spend much time in Tooting, and I couldn't imagine that he came to Fort Doom much, either.

Then something strange happened. Tariq was asking him about the place and saying how wonderful it was when Leo glanced around him – at the piano and the dancers – and suddenly said in a loud, clear voice, 'All right, Hal, you can stop that now.'

There was silence for a moment and then a voice that made me jump said: 'Stop what?'

Obviously it must have come from hidden speakers, but it seemed to come from all over the place, like it was the building itself talking.

'You know very well,' said Leo, in the same loud voice. 'Stop the tea dance and serve us some tea.'

'When you say "tea,"' said the other voice, the voice from the walls, 'do you mean a cup of tea or the whole works?'

The voice was deep and rich and very English – like warm gravy. A bit like an English butler, but not quite so polite. There was a sarcastic edge to it. Like the voice on Dad's satnav. You could imagine it saying, 'Which of the words "Turn" and "Right" did you not understand?'

We were all standing around listening to this, and smiling awkwardly, like when people have an argument in public. All of us except Mei, of course, who was just looking bored, like she heard it all the time.

'Would you like a proper tea?' said Leo, in his normal voice, looking at us all.

We nodded. Personally I wasn't sure that I did want a proper tea – I was too nervous – but it seemed the easiest option.

'The whole works,' said Leo, raising his voice again. 'In my apartment.'

And so off we go to Leo's apartment.

It was in the tower that was furthest out from the shore, and we had to go round the cinema and the gym towers to reach it, over the catwalks and up and down several ladders: Leo in the lead with Tariq behind him, then me and Nina, and then Mei and Ella bringing up the rear. It took us about five minutes. The catwalks were solid enough but it was a bit unnerving to walk all that way over the sea – and climbing the ladders was worse. And this was a calm, sunny day. It must have been amazing in a storm. Even though the towers had stood for seventy years, you'd be worried this was going to be the storm that finally brought them crashing into the sea. At least I would be.

There was a part of me that couldn't believe this was happening. That it was like the dream about the fire. Totally vivid and believable and scary as hell, but not *real*. But finally we reached the tower where Leo had his apartment.

The door was made of steel like all the others in the fort and there was a camera above it. Leo stood in front of it and looked up.

'OK, Hal,' he said. 'It's me.'

'Who's me?' said the voice.

'Don't be boring, Hal. You know who I am. Open the door.'

'What's the password?'

Leo looked back at us. 'Silly game time,' he said.

Then he turned round again. 'Hal, if you don't open this sodding door I'm going to get my pump-action shotgun and I'm going to blow so many holes in you, we'll be able to use you to drain lettuce.'

There was a small silence. 'That would be very foolish of you,' said Hal.

But the door opened.

And we stepped into what looked like the Great Hall of a medieval castle. The place where the baron does his entertaining. I recognized it from the history we were doing at school. There was no proper ceiling, just a roof, way up above our heads, supported by lots of heavy black beams, and a gallery halfway up the wall at the far end, like a minstrels' gallery. There were big heavy tapestries hanging on the walls and old-fashioned weapons and shields everywhere. And there were all these suits of armour, standing along the walls like sentries. At least, I assume they were suits of armour and there was no one in them, but I wouldn't have been that surprised if there were. There was a great stone fireplace with lots of carvings on it that looked like dragons or demons. And in the middle of the room there was a table – set for tea.

I'd never seen a tea like it. This was the whole works all right. There were plates and plates of sandwiches, two large cakes – one chocolate, one iced – dozens of smaller cakes on cake stands, hot buttered scones, silver bowls of strawberry jam, more silver bowls full of cream, tons of chocolate biscuits, two large pots of tea and two jugs of fruit juice. There was even a jelly – I mean, who makes jellies any more? I didn't know what it was at first; it was shaped like a large yellow seashell. And there was this fantastic tea service with lots of delicate little china cups and saucers and plates with dragons all over them.

We stood there looking at it.

'Not bad,' says Leo. Then he raised his voice like he had before. 'Thank you, Hal.'

'Don't mention it,' said the voice, but still with that hint of sarcasm. 'Any time.'

I looked at Nina and I could see she was thinking the same thing I was. No computer could have done this, no matter how advanced. This must be Leo's idea of a joke. Either he had staff here all along, or the helicopter had brought them in. But there was no sign of them. If they were here they'd been kept well out of sight.

We sat around the table. There was a moment when I felt like you do at a race when you're waiting for the starting pistol. Then I went for it.

I wolfed down a plate of sandwiches – tuna, ham, cheese and chutney, smoked salmon. Then I started on the cakes.

It's a funny thing but I can be nervous as anything, with my stomach so churned up that the very thought of food is enough to make me feel like throwing up – then someone sticks a plate in front of me, and I'm away. It comes of playing football, I think. But there is a theory that I'm just plain greedy.

'There's a girl with a healthy appetite,' said Ella. She looked quite shocked.

I saw Leo looking at me with an approving smile on his face, though, so I knew it was all right. I wondered if he had any kids of his own. There'd been nothing about it in any of the things I'd read about him. He was older than I'd thought, though – probably about the same age as Tariq, but not so grey. He probably dyes it, I thought.

The two of them were sitting at the far end of the table a little bit distanced from the rest of us and doing more talking than eating. I couldn't hear what they were saying but I guessed it must be about the conference and I was a bit annoyed that they didn't bring us into it. I think even at this point I was getting a bit edgy that the whole thing was going to be taken over by adults. But Leo kept looking at me from time to time and even Tariq was, so that I wondered if they were talking about me.

Then, when we'd finished, Leo suggested we go downstairs. I thought this was going to be his office or something and we were going to talk business, but after what I'd seen so far I should have known better.

It was only a bit smaller than the hall and it was like a film set. In fact, at first I thought it *was* a film set. I recognized at least half a dozen things I'd seen on television or in movies. There was a Dalek from 'Dr Who' and a life-size model of Buckbeak from Harry Potter, and several large chess pieces I was sure I'd seen in *Alice in Wonderland*.

You really didn't know where to look next. There were all these model aircraft hanging from the ceiling and older stuff like steam engines and toy soldiers and animals all over the floor. There was even a fairground carousel with all these horses and dragons on it, and a castle – a huge fantasy castle about the size of a garden shed – with one army on the battlements and another outside laying siege to it with catapults. There were so many things you couldn't take them all in. Some things were still in their boxes. It was like a kid's bedroom where nothing was ever put away, except it was the size of a football pitch. Leo called it his den.

He really was like a big kid. I'd read somewhere that he hadn't had much of a childhood – he was one of five kids and their dad had left them when Leo was very young. Their mum was depressed and couldn't work so they all had to do jobs to bring in some money, even from an early age. When Leo was eight he'd had a paper round, he'd washed people's cars in a supermarket car park, and he'd run all kinds of money-making scams at school. He said he'd had to grow up too fast.

He was making up for it now all right. He had this model racetrack all round the room, like Scalextric except that the cars were really old-fashioned and didn't have metal conductors underneath; they used batteries which stopped as soon as they crashed or ran off the track. Leo made us all race against him one after the other – except Mei, who refused to play; she said Leo always won by miles. He did, too, even when he gave us a start of half a lap.

He had this gallery halfway up the wall, like the minstrels' gallery in the Great Hall, except that it had a glass front so you could look down on the whole thing. Leo called it the control room. Pretty soon we were almost as excited as he was – it was hard not to be with all the energy he put into it, and all the yelling and shouting. It was great fun, but I couldn't help thinking this wasn't actually why we'd come here, and maybe Leo picked this up, because after he'd won for about the tenth time he suddenly looked a bit sheepish and said, 'OK, I suppose we'd better get down to business.'

So we did.

He wanted to know what had given me the idea in the first place so I told him about the Children's Crusade. I even told him about the Pied Piper. He said he liked the idea of that. I didn't tell him about the Spook, though, and that I thought I only had a couple of years to live. I thought that would be too weird, even for him. Then he wanted to know exactly what we had in mind and what we were going to talk about at the conference.

'That depends on the delegates,' I said. 'It's what *they* want to talk about. Not me.'

He nodded as if he approved of that. But then he said, 'So are they just going to talk, or are you going to do something?'

I didn't know how to answer that, but Tariq went on about drawing up an action plan and setting targets and holding people to them. Leo was half listening to him, still smiling, but I thought there was a glint in his eye. He was probably thinking about submarines and torpedoes.

'It's not people,' he said. 'People aren't the problem.'

'I mean people in power,' said Tariq.

'People in power!' Leo curled his lip scornfully. 'What are they going to do for you? It's like the story of the Pied Piper. They'll promise the world when they want something. But when they get it, you can go sing for it.'

I thought that would be it, then. That he'd wish us the best of luck and send us packing and carry on doing things his way, whatever that was.

Then he looked at me and he said: 'What do your folks think of all this?'

'My folks?' I said. I knew what he meant but I was a bit taken aback.

'Your mum and dad.'

'Oh, they're all for it,' I said.

Now this wasn't entirely true. For a start my dad was away again and as far as I knew, he didn't know anything about it. I'd mentioned it to Mum, but I'd been a bit vague about it. I'd just told her it was an environmental project we were doing at school. If I'd said it was my own idea, she'd only have worried that it was going to interfere with my homework. You should hear the way she goes on about football. Besides, I didn't really think anything would come of it.

'And do they know *I'm* involved?' he said.

'Not really,' I said. I'd told Mum that Tariq was taking us to see someone who was going to help with our project. Which was true. There was no point in telling Mum it was Leo Lyall because even if she was listening she'd probably never heard of him and if she had she wouldn't believe me.

'Not really?' Leo repeated, looking at me with his head to one side and a funny expression on his face.

'Well, you're not involved, are you?' I said. 'Yet.' It came out a bit sharper than I'd meant it to. I saw Nina wince and Tariq was stroking his beard, which is always a bad sign.

'Oh, I'm involved,' Leo said. 'I'm very involved. I'll be involved just as much as you want me to be. Maybe more.'

He gave me a look that should have worried me a bit, thinking back on it, but at the time we were too excited to worry about anything. Leo told Tariq his people would be in touch about putting money into the project and that in the meantime we could use his name as a sponsor. He'd even appear on the opening day of the conference and the band could introduce it, if we wanted, with something from 'Requiem for a Dying Planet'.

Suddenly it looked like it was all go. Tariq gave me a hug, grinning away like he'd won the Lottery, and Ella was going through diaries with Mei to organize our next meeting. Then I noticed Leo watching me again in a way that made me a bit nervous. I had the same feeling I'd had at the heliport, that I was getting into something that was way, way too deep for me to handle. But I told myself I was just being pathetic. We'd got everything we wanted.

Leo came out onto the helicopter pad to see us off and when we looked down we saw him standing all alone on the empty platform in his long black coat, not waving or anything, even though we were waving at him, but just looking at us, with his coat and his long hair blowing in the wind. I suddenly felt sad about him, because he seemed such a lonely figure and I felt bad that we were leaving him there, in his deserted old fort. I imagined him going back inside and playing with his racing cars all by himself.

I know it was probably just an act and that he was probably never alone – and even if he was it would be his own choice – but even so, I felt there was a sadness, a loneliness about him that never really went away. And that this was why he'd bought Fort Doom, because it was like him. Isolated and abandoned, and a bit out of this world.

You'll say how could I tell what he was like, just from that one short meeting? But I felt that I did, and that we had something in common.

I felt a bit miserable going back to Balham. Not that I've got anything against Balham. It's got a lot of advantages over an abandoned fort in the Thames Estuary. Like Sainsbury's and Waitrose and Poundsavers. And Balham Library. And you can get almost anywhere from Balham Station. But even so. I felt I'd had a taste of something different, like when you read a book about somewhere strange and wild and adventurous and you feel a bit flat when you get to the last page and look out the window and see the same old street and the same old houses, and it's raining.

Then I got home and found my dad was back.

And boy, was I in trouble.

14

Conversation with a Ghost

'Did you know about this?'

This is my dad to my mum when I get back from Fort Doom.

No 'Did you have a good trip? What was it like?' No 'You went by helicopter? To a fort in the Thames Estuary? Cool. And you met Leo Lyall? Wow.'

'I most certainly did *not* know,' says Mum, glaring at me.

'Well, I told you,' I said, glaring back.

'You most certainly did *not* tell me.'

'I most certainly did,' I said. I waited for her to say 'I most certainly did not' again, but she didn't, which was a pity because I could keep this going for at least as long as she could.

'When?' she said.

'Last night.'

'When last night?'

'When I got home from school.'

'You told me Tariq was picking you up to take you somewhere with Nina. Something to do with this environment thing you're doing. You said nothing whatsoever about going up in a *helicopter* – and you *certainly* said nothing about *you-know-who*.'

You-know-who?

'You mean Leo Lyall?'

'Yes. Who else?' But she looked a bit guilty, as if she wasn't quite so sure of herself now.

'I'm sure I did,' I said. 'You just can't have heard me.'

This is a good one to throw at my mother because she's often in the middle of something and she doesn't hear what you're saying to her. Or if she hears, she doesn't take it in. It goes in one ear and out the other. You just have to pick the right moment.

'She'd have heard you,' said my dad quietly.

I saw her shoot him a look. I was really puzzled by all of this. I didn't even think they'd have heard of Leo Lyall. It's not their kind of music. But something's obviously got to them. She's in a strop and he's . . .

I don't know. He might have been speaking quietly but I could tell he was really mad at me. I didn't know what was the matter with him. Or her. I mean, I expected them to be surprised, but not angry. What had I done to deserve this? I'm standing there in the kitchen like I'm on trial or something.

'Well, we didn't know for sure that he'd be there,' I said.

'So you *didn't* tell me,' said Mum, triumphantly.

'I can't remember if I mentioned him *personally*,' I said. I had an inspiration. 'It would be like showing off. But what does it matter, anyway?'

'It matters that you're not honest with us,' said my dad.

'What do you mean, I'm not honest with you?' I was getting indignant now. 'I haven't told lies. I haven't made anything up.'

'There's such a thing as the sin of omission,' he said.

What's he on about? The sin of omission? I went on the attack. 'You weren't there,' I said. 'How do you know what I said to her?'

'That'll do, Kit,' said Mum, in the voice she uses when she's warning you not to push it and she's just a step or two away from declaring war. And believe me, you do not want my mum declaring war on you.

'Well I just don't see what the fuss is about,' I said. I was close to tears now because it was so unfair, and maybe because deep down I knew I should have been a bit more open about it. But it had all happened so quickly. I didn't know about the helicopter until I got in Tariq's car and he told me, and I really hadn't expected to meet Leo Lyall. I thought we'd just be meeting one of his publicity people or something. I wasn't going to go on about meeting this famous rock star and then have to come home and say he wasn't there.

'It's not as if I went off by myself to meet some weirdo,' I said. 'I was with Tariq and Nina. And it wasn't like we were sneaking off to some rock concert or something. We were trying to get him to give us some support. For something really important. And we did. And all I get from you two is *this*.'

I started to stalk off then. I know a good exit line when I hear it. I just don't often get to think of one.

'Sit down, Kit,' says my dad.

'No,' I said.

'Sit down,' he said.

I sat down.

But I folded my arms to let him know I wasn't happy about it.

'OK,' he said, 'so tell us exactly what's going on here.'

'I've told you . . .' I began.

'Well, tell us again,' he said. 'Now you've got our undivided attention. What exactly is this conference thing, whose idea was it, and why is what's-his-face involved?'

What's-his-face? You-know-who? Why couldn't they say his name? It was like he was the Devil, or something, or the Dark Lord – He-Who-Must-Not-Be-Named.

I told them. Again. As much as I wanted them to know.

I didn't tell them this was something I wanted to do before I died, of course, and that I only had two or three years to fit it in. But I was tempted, the way they were treating me.

'So that's it,' I said. 'I'd have thought you'd be pleased. I'd have thought you'd want to be supportive. Not give me a hard time.'

'Oh Kit,' said my mum, shaking her head.

'Did you really not know about this?' Dad says to her.

'I thought it was some school thing,' she said. 'I'm sure that's what you told me,' she said to me.

'You never listen,' I said. I thought I'd get my own back a bit.

'Well, I think it's a very . . . creditable idea,' said my dad, 'but if you want us to be supportive, you might at least have discussed it with us first.'

'How can I discuss it with you when you're never here?' I said.

'OK, OK.' He was looking so hurt I wished I hadn't said that now, but it definitely gave me the advantage. 'But I'm here now,' he said, 'and there's a few things that need to be sorted.'

'Like what?' I said.

'Like is it going to involve you in a load of work? Is it going to interfere with your schoolwork? Are you going to be flying off all the time to meet people like – you know, Mr Cool.'

There it was again.

'What have you got against him?' I said. 'Why can't you even say his name?'

'Well, he's not exactly the most *sane* person in the universe.'

'Who says?' I'm not forgetting I'd pretty well said the same thing myself not so very long ago, but

I hadn't met him then.

'Most people over the age of about seven,' says Dad nastily.

'Tariq's over seven and he didn't seem to think so,' I snapped back.

'Have you asked him?'

'No, but—'

'Look, I know you think we're just a couple of old misery guts, and I'm the last person to go all sanctimonious on you, I hope, but, you know, if only half the things people say about him are true, he's a bit, well, flaky.'

'Flaky?' I said, screwing my face up as if I didn't know what he meant. In fact, I'd have put it a lot stronger than flaky myself.

'Mad, bad and dangerous to know,' said Mum softly. It sounded like she was quoting someone. Dad was looking at her but she was staring down at the table.

'Well, he was OK with me,' I said.

She looked up sharply. Dad looked away. He seemed to be holding himself in check.

'What do you mean?' says Mum. 'What did he say to you?'

'Nothing much,' I shrugged. 'He was just . . .

friendly. He even asked me what my mum and dad thought about it.'

'Great,' said Dad, meaning the opposite. He was still staring at the kitchen wall.

'Well, at least he cares about things,' I said. 'Not like some people.'

He looked at me then. 'What things?'

'He cares about what's happening to the planet, he cares about people . . .'

'People,' he snorted.

'He obviously cares about what my parents think . . .'

'He cares about himself, Kit.' He wasn't speaking quietly now; he was practically shouting. 'He doesn't give that about people.' He clicked his fingers. 'He's totally wrapped up in himself. He's a druggie, he's warped, he's violent, he's been in and out of prison, he's a foul-mouthed, aggressive, arrogant son of a . . .' he struggled to think of a word he felt he could use in his own home in front of his eleven-year-old daughter. He should stand around in the Waverley playground for a minute or so – that'd give him a few ideas.

'He speaks very highly of you, too,' I said.

I honestly don't know what put those words in my

head. It was like someone else speaking them. Someone sneering and horrid.

Dad looked at me for a second, then he stood up and walked out of the room.

I caught my mother's eye.

'Oh Kit,' she says, shaking her head sadly at me, 'you have no idea what you've done.'

I sat in my room staring at a blank computer screen for about half an hour. I'd started to play 'Football Manager' to take my mind off things but I couldn't concentrate.

You have no idea what you've done.

What was she on about?

Honestly, my parents – I sometimes feel like giving up on them, but where else would I live? Nina's? Fort Doom?

I thought about what it must be like to live there, like a modern princess in a tower. It had its attractions, but there were too many things I'd miss. Football, for one. Playing with model racing cars for hours on end was no real substitute.

Besides, my parents would never let me. They'd really got a thing about Leo Lyall. What was that all about? I know a lot of parents have it in for rock stars but my parents aren't usually like that. This seemed like it was almost personal.

Normally, I'd have rung Nina to talk it over with her, but I knew she was at some family thing and I didn't want her to get into trouble for talking to me for hours on end on the phone. She has to be on her best behaviour when she's with Tariq's family because he says he doesn't want them to know how badly she's been brought up. I thought about my other friends but there was no one else I could talk to like I talk to Nina. So in the end I just mooched around in my room for the rest of the evening playing 'Football Manager' on the computer and doing stuff on Facebook.

The funny thing is I didn't tell anyone about Leo Lyall. I don't know why. For once I had something really interesting to tell people and I didn't say a word. I thought about it. I even tried it out. I wrote it on my Wall.

Spent the day with Leo Lyall on his fort on the Thames.

Then I deleted it. Who was going to believe me? I'd let Nina tell people and they could call *her* a liar. Besides, after what Mum and Dad had said it didn't seem so special any more – they'd spoiled it for me in a way. And I just didn't know why.

Leo Lyall might be all the things Dad said he was but I didn't think that was the real reason he was so mad at me. I thought it was more to do with what was going on between him and Mum, as if he blamed her for something: probably the way I was being brought up. But if he was that bothered, why didn't he spend more time at home? They might as well get divorced, the amount of time they spend together.

I felt so miserable and lonely I could have wept. I started thinking about the Spook again. I hadn't seen her for ages, not since I'd had the idea about the children's conference. I switched the light off and crossed over to the window.

Nothing. Just the empty street. Not even a fox. I was about to let the curtain fall back and then I saw her.

She was standing under one of the streetlights on the Common, the same as before, staring up at the house. She was wearing her emo gear. Leather jacket, boots – it was Saturday night, after all. Maybe she was on her way out. But she wasn't moving. Just standing there looking up at me.

Suddenly I knew I had to go and talk to her. I checked the time. 7.30. I didn't have an excuse for going out, not in the dark at that time of night, but

I could always sneak out the back door, just for a few minutes. They wouldn't know I'd gone.

I crept down the stairs as quietly as I could. I could hear the TV on and there was a light in the sitting room. I peered through the crack in the door. I could see Dad in there, with his feet up, watching the football on television. It made me sad because normally I'd be in there with him and we'd be watching the football together. I peeped into the kitchen. Mum was on her hands and knees with her back to me, cleaning the oven. Cleaning the oven on a Saturday night – can you believe it? And Dad's just back from a trip. I could have screamed at her. Or him.

But instead I crept back down the hall and slid open the latch on the front door. Then I remembered my keys. I'd need them to get back in again. I crept back up the stairs, freezing every time one of them creaked. The keys were on my dressing-room table. I sneaked a look out of the window again. The Spook was still there. I had a feeling she was waiting for me.

I let myself out the front door and closed it quietly behind me. It was only then that I wondered what I was going to say.

How do you talk to a ghost? If she *was* a ghost.

I remembered what she'd said to me last time, when I was lying in the road with the bike wrapped round my legs.

But I took a deep breath and walked up to her. She was dressed more or less the same as that first time, but her face was different. It seemed even whiter, and there was a single line of red, like blood, dripping down from her bottom lip. And she was smoking.

She looked at me, in a sneering kind of way, smoke curling from her lips.

'Hi,' I said. 'How's it going?'

She said something rude.

'I'm sorry,' I said, 'I just saw you standing here and I thought . . .'

'What? That I was waiting for you?'

'Well . . .'

'Don't flatter yourself, kid.'

'So why . . .' I looked around us. The road was deserted, which was a bit odd because it was Saturday night, about the time most people were going out. There were dark clouds, like rags, scudding across the moon and there was a hint of rain in the air.

'I'm just hanging out,' she shrugged. Then she blew smoke in my face.

I stepped back. I hate that: people blowing smoke in your face. I hate smoking generally, especially kids smoking, and she was a kid, whatever she might like to think about it. For a moment I really hated her. With her white make-up and her piercings and the blood-red line dripping down from her mouth. She was obviously going for the vampire look, which is so yesterday.

'Who *are* you?' I said.

'Don't you know?' she sneered.

Honestly, I could have slapped her, even if she was a head taller than me and about twice as heavy, but I was afraid my hand would go straight through her.

'Why are you so horrible?' I said. She just leered at me. 'How did you *get* like this?'

'Why are you so horrible; how did you get like this?' she repeated in a whiny voice that was nothing like mine. 'Good question. Why do you think?'

I didn't say anything. What could I say? I just stood there biting my lip. This was ridiculous. She looked so solid – she had to be real. I looked behind me again, towards our house. That was real enough. The light was on above the front door, and there was another light in the sitting room where Dad was watching television.

'How are they getting on?' she said.

I turned back to her. 'What?' I said. But I was really scared now. It was as if she knew.

'Them,' she said, jerking her head in the direction of our house. 'She still cleaning the oven?'

I could feel the blood draining from my face. I was probably as white as she was. How could she have known?

'Clean, clean, clean,' she said. 'Dust, dust, dust. Have you ever thought what she's *really* cleaning? What she's *trying* to clean?'

'Leave her alone,' I said. I was clenching my fists.

'And what about him?' she said. 'What's *he* doing? Watching television – or on the phone to one of his girlfriends?'

I was stunned. It was like she'd hit me. She made that sound again, that could have been a laugh. Then she walked away.

I was still standing there with my fist clenched. But she hadn't finished with me yet. She had one parting shot.

'Oh, and say hello to Daddy,' she said, looking back over her shoulder, 'next time he sends his helicopter for you.'

15

The Magic Number

What did she mean – '*Say hello to Daddy?*'

I stood there, long after she'd gone, thinking about it. And all the other things she'd said. It began to rain. There were people walking past. Funny – they weren't there when I was talking to the Spook, but now the street seemed to be full of them, on their way out for the evening.

Two of them had stopped and were staring at me from the other side of the road. I knew them. Simon and Jenny. They lived a few doors away. They've got a cute two-year-old kid called Jamie but they must have got a babysitter for the night. They crossed over to me.

'Kit? Are you all right?'

'Yes,' I said. 'I'm fine.' I was trying not to cry. 'I was just — I was looking for the cat.'

'Oh,' said Jenny. 'I didn't know you had a cat.'

'It's not ours,' I said. 'We're just looking after it.'

That's the thing with lies. Once you start you have to keep going, digging a deeper hole for yourself.

They looked round as if they were looking for it too. 'What's it called?' said Jenny.

'Spook,' I said.

'Spook? Funny name for a cat.' They looked out into the Common, as if it might be lurking there. I hadn't noticed how dark it was until now.

'It's a black cat,' I said. 'Spook!' I shouted. 'Here puss. Puss, puss, puss.'

I thought I heard a sound from out of the darkness. It could have been the cry of a fox — or the Spook laughing.

'You're getting wet,' said Simon.

'Do your mum and dad know you're out in the rain?' said Jenny.

'No,' I said. 'I'd better get back.' But I didn't move. I didn't want to go back. But where else could I go? I couldn't even go to Nina's, cos she was with her family.

'I think you should,' said Jenny. 'It'll come back of its own accord, when it gets wet enough.'

'But what if a fox gets it?' I said.

'Have you seen the foxes around here?' said Simon. 'A cat'd make mincemeat of them.'

They escorted me back to the gate and watched while I let myself in the front door.

'Tom?' I heard Mum's voice from the kitchen. 'Is that you?'

I didn't say anything but as I was heading for the stairs she comes out into the hallway. She stared at me in astonishment.

'Kit? What on earth . . . ? You're soaked to the skin. What were you doing outside?'

'I went for a walk,' I said.

'What do you mean, you went for a walk? What – on your own, in the rain?'

I walked past her and started up the stairs.

'Kit! I'm talking to you. Since when did you go outside without telling us?'

I kept on going. When I looked back from the top of the stairs Dad was standing there too. They were both staring up at me, as if I was a ghost.

Next day Nina rang. 'Your mum's been on,' she said.

'She spoke to my mum and then to my dad. What's going on?'

'Nothing,' I said.

'What do you mean, nothing? It can't be nothing. Is it about Leo Lyall?'

'Sort of,' I said.

'Well, what about him?'

'Didn't they tell you?'

'No. You know what they're like. They said it's none of my business.'

'They don't like him,' I said.

'What?'

'Mum and Dad. They don't like Leo Lyall. They don't want me to have anything more to do with him.'

A small silence. Then she said, 'Why not?'

'Oh, you know. They said he's mad.'

Mad, bad and dangerous to know.

'Yeah, well, so what?'

'Try telling them that.'

'So what are you going to do?'

'Nothing,' I said.

'So . . . are you going to give up on the idea? The conference and everything?'

'No,' I said. It was the first time I'd thought about

it, but I knew I wasn't going to give it up. 'Why should I?'

Another small silence. Then she said: 'Can you come round?'

'No,' I said. 'I'm grounded.'

'Do you want me to come round to you?'

'No,' I said. 'I'll see you tomorrow in school.'

I wasn't ready to tell her what the Spook had told me. I needed to think about it first.

I thought about it for the rest of the day. It didn't get me very far. She was obviously not to be trusted. She was full of spite and malice; anyone could see that.

But what if she was me? A later version of me, in a couple of years' time, maybe, just before I died?

How had I got like that?

If I was going to turn out like that, I'd rather be dead.

But she couldn't possibly be me. She was some twisted psycho, pretending to be me. My doppelgänger. She was probably having a good laugh about it with her mates.

But then I thought about what she'd said about Mum cleaning the oven. How could she have known that?

Clean, clean, clean. Dust, dust, dust. Have you ever thought what she's really cleaning? What she's trying to clean?

And then there was the stuff about my dad.

Watching television – or on the phone to one of his girlfriends?

I think that's what bothered me most of all. I'd thought about it, of course. All the time he spent away. The atmosphere at home. One or two things that had been said. But I'd put it to the back of my mind. It wasn't something you wanted to think about.

I stayed in my room most of the day, pretending to do my homework.

Mum and Dad came up to see me. Separately. I didn't tell them anything. I could see they were worried, but they thought I was sulking because of what they'd said about Leo Lyall and the conference. I let them sweat. It would do them good.

We had Sunday lunch together but it was horrible. No one speaking. Afterwards I watched the football. Even that couldn't cheer me up. Fulham v. Queen's Park Rangers. Great.

When I went to school on Monday I could see Nina was dying to tell me something. She had to wait until the mid-morning break.

Mum had been onto Tariq and they'd worked something out. I could carry on with the conference so long as I didn't have anything to do with Leo Lyall. And there was going to be a steering committee – to take the weight off my shoulders.

'What's a steering committee?' I said, suspiciously.

'It does all the organizing,' she said. 'You'll be on it. And so will I. But there'll be others.'

'What others?' I was still suspicious.

'Other kids. We can pick them ourselves. So long as they're from Years Seven and Eight.'

I looked around the playground. 'From here?' I said.

She shrugged. 'If we like.'

We went back to Nina's after school. Nina had got hold of a list of names for the whole of Years Seven and Eight – I don't know how. She said we should make a shortlist and then interview them. Her dad had said we should make them as international as possible.

It wasn't difficult. At the first school assembly the head had said there were forty-four different languages spoken at Waverley. He was quite proud of it.

So we went through the list. We hardly knew any of them, of course, just the ones in our own class and a few others we'd known from the last school, or those I knew who were in the Year Seven football team. I wanted to choose from them, but Nina wouldn't let me.

'We need to be selective,' she said.

I knew Nina's method of selecting. I'd done this with her once before, when we were at Pinewood. We'd written this play about Robin Hood – except that it was called *Robina Hood and Her Merrie Women* – and Miss Havelock said we could do it with the class, and if it was good enough we could perform it in front of the whole school and the parents at the end-of-term assembly. The only problem was, everyone in the class had to have a part.

Even after we'd cast Robina Hood and Maid Marion and all the Merrie Women and the Sheriff of Nottingham and all his trained hooligans, we still had about fifteen kids left over who hadn't got any parts. All boys.

So Nina goes, 'They can be peasants.'

'What do you have to do if you're a peasant?' I asked her.

'Well, you just wear a smock and stand around and go *Arrr*,' she says. 'Or you collect sticks in the forest.'

And that gave her another idea. She decided some kids could be trees.

'What do you do if you're a tree?' I said.

'You just stand around with your arms in the air wearing a brown apron with a green paper bag over your head. And then when the wind blows you wave your arms about and go *Whoooo*.'

So we went through all the names that were left over, with Nina going, 'Peasant' or 'Tree'.

I didn't think they'd be very impressed being a Peasant or a Tree but they loved it. They had a much better time than anyone else in the play going *Arrrr* and *Whoooo* all the time and waving their arms about.

But this time it was much more difficult. We had to pick people who were interested in climate change. And it wasn't easy.

'You'd think,' said Nina after a while, 'that with 500 names to choose from we could come up with five who want to save the planet.'

'Why five?' I said.

'Because with you and me that makes seven,' she said.

I was no wiser. 'So – why seven?' I said.

'Because seven is a magic number,' she tells me.

Don't ask. I didn't. Sometimes it's better to just let Nina have her way or you'll be there all night.

So we decided to advertise. We put a note up on the school noticeboard. Nina wrote it.

Calling All Year 7/8 Students Who Want To Save the Planet!!!!!

A preliminary meeting will be held in the School Library

on Monday October 1st at 12.30 p.m.

All those attending will receive a free ticket to

Leo Lyall's next concert!!!!!!

I made her take out the last line, but otherwise I thought it was a big improvement on how we'd selected kids for *Robina Hood and Her Merrie Women*.

Four kids turned up. Nina blamed me.

'Well, that cuts down on the decision-making,' she said.

Their names were:

Nicky Adebayo

Lucy Mandela

Li Ching

and

Amor Gagalac.

'Should keep Dad happy,' said Nina. 'Two African names, one from China and I don't know where Amor's from – probably Venus.' It turned out to be the Philippines.

'There's only one boy,' I pointed out.

'Can't be helped,' said Nina briskly. 'Besides, it's

boys who got us into this mess in the first place.'

'Sorry?'

'The mess the world's in,' she says. 'You can't blame girls for it. How many women run multinational companies? How many women run banks? How many women run governments?'

'Right,' I said. 'But what about the magic number?'

'We'll just have to live without it,' she says. 'Or we can look for someone later.'

But then we had a problem with Li Ching. He said if he was the only boy he was out of here.

'What a wuss!' said Nina.

'OK, I'm walking,' said Li, heading for the door.

'Hang on,' I said, glaring at Nina. I asked him if he had any friends he could bring. He thought about it. He decided there might be one. He was French and he was in Year Seven. His name was Raoul Le Blanc.

'Another great name!' says Nina. 'We'll have him.'

But she couldn't find him on her list.

'He only started last week,' said Li. 'His parents just moved here from Paris.'

'So how do you know him?' Nina demanded.

'He's joined the tennis club.' Li was a tennis freak. 'He's got a great serve.'

'It's not much of a qualification for saving the planet,' I said.

Nina gave me a look. 'Pick, pick, pick,' she said. 'What do you want, a degree in climatology? Get him in,' she says to Li.

So we got him in. To give us our magic number.

He was quite good looking – well, in fact he was very good looking. Long dark hair, and brown eyes and brown skin. But I can't say I took to him at first. I thought he was too pleased with himself, a bit stuck up. I thought, he's the sort of boy who thinks he's irresistible. Like Omar. And there was the name. Raoul Le Blanc. I mean. No wonder I thought he was pleased with himself.

But it turned out he was just shy. He had this lovely shy smile. I think that's what made me decide he couldn't be all that bad.

He was just a couple of months short of his thirteenth birthday, about a year older than me. His name – I looked it up later – meant Wolf Boy in English, or Wolf Counsellor. Raoul. Say it aloud. It sounds like a soft growl.

The only thing I really had against him was that he didn't like football. He was into rugby. His parents came from the South of France, apparently, and it's what they play down there. I decided I could live with this.

And the really great thing was, he seemed to like me.

In fact, and I know this sounds like I'm full of myself, but I think this was the main reason he joined the group. It was the way he kept catching my eye and smiling that shy smile, as if we had some private joke going.

The meeting went quite well, too. We set ourselves up as a steering committee with Nina in the chair and me as secretary. Then we drew up a mission statement. Nina more or less dictated it but we all voted in favour:

This committee resolves to invite Delegates from all over the World to attend the
International Children's Conference on the Environment
to draw up a **Plan of Action** to present to the United Nations, World Leaders and Heads of Government, Industry, Finance and Commerce to Secure the Future of the Planet.
Children of the World Unite!

The meeting was at the end of the day and afterwards we were hanging about outside, still talking about what we've decided and how we're going to do it, and people were drifting off, and Nina asked if I was coming back to her place.

'No, I have to go home,' I said. 'They want to talk to me.' I pulled a face.

I didn't know what they wanted to talk about but I wasn't looking forward to it.

'OK. See you tomorrow,' says Nina.

And I suddenly find there's just me and Raoul.

We looked at each other. Oh my God!

'Which way are you going?' I said.

'Across the Common,' he says.

It turns out he lives just a couple of streets away from where I live. So we're walking back across the Common together, just the two of us, and I'm thinking, whatever you do, don't say anything stupid. I was thinking about the time I'd been with Omar and I'd asked him about his groin. The trouble is, once I'd got that in my mind, I couldn't think of anything else. All you have to do is keep your mouth shut, I'm thinking. Just listen to him talking and smile and nod. It's not too much to ask.

But the trouble was, he wasn't talking either.

We're just walking along in this total silence and it gets worse and worse with every step until I break out in a cold sweat; I think I'm going to scream.

I've got to say something. Anything. As long as it's not about groins.

'Oh, there's a squirrel hiding its nuts,' I said.

Oh please! *Please*. Dear God, open the earth and swallow me up.

That bloody, bloody squirrel; I could have killed it. I think it must have sensed this because it took one look at me and ran up a tree, taking its nuts with it.

But today something was on my side, because Raoul started to speak at the same time. You know how it happens sometimes? When no one's saying anything and then you both speak at once. I've no idea what he said. It didn't matter. All that mattered was that he can't have heard what I'd said about the squirrel and its nuts.

'Sorry, go on,' he said.

'No, you go on,' I said.

'No, you. Please.'

I was so glad Nina wasn't with us. But if she had been it wouldn't have happened, cos she'd have done all the talking.

'I was just going to say . . .' What? *What??????*

I had no idea. My mind was a total blank. I can feel him looking at me, waiting. Squirrels, nuts, Omar's strained groin . . . 'Do you like living in England?' I said.

It came out a bit loud, a bit desperate – even angry, as if I was trying to pick a fight. He was looking quite startled.

Then he grinned and it was like the sun coming out. 'I do now,' he said.

It was just as well I was blushing already. Of course, he might not mean *me*. He might mean anything. He might just mean because he's made some friends, he's joined a gang, he's found something useful to do, he's saving the planet.

'Why did you come here?' I said, just to say something. 'I mean, why did your parents come here?'

'My father, he come here for his job,' he said. Well, this was more or less obvious but I'm in nodding and smiling mode now. Much safer. 'He is architect.'

His English wasn't that brilliant, but we were up and running now, talking about family, friends, people generally. He asked me what my dad did and when I told him, he seemed really interested, not just pretending. It turned out this was one of the things Raoul wanted to be – a photographer. Or rather, a cameraman. He was into movies.

'Do you like the movies?' he said.

'Yeah,' I said, but a bit as if I could take them or leave them. I was a bit distracted, to be honest. I was wondering if he was going to ask me to go out with him, to see a movie.

But then he said: 'You do not want to be a photographer, like your father?'

'Not really,' I said. 'I'd rather be a footballer.'

He was looking puzzled. 'Do girls play the football in England?' he asked.

This was usually enough to start me off, but this time I didn't. I just said: 'Well, not many girls make a living out of it. But it might change – in the future.'

And then suddenly I remembered. I didn't have a future.

It hit me like a blow. I mean, for the first time in days I hadn't been thinking about it. And for the first time, I knew how much I wanted to live. I almost burst into tears.

Fortunately Raoul didn't notice. We're still walking on.

'But your big interest, it is to save the world,' he said.

'Sort of,' I said dully. And then I made up my

mind. I was going to stop worrying about what was going to happen to me in the future. I was just going to live for now. And I was going to stop worrying about the Spook. Maybe Nina was right. Maybe it was all in the mind. Maybe if I refused to believe in her she'd go away. And why was I so convinced she was me?

'There is something wrong?' said Raoul. He's looking at me a bit anxiously.

'No,' I said. 'Why?'

'The way you look,' he said. He turned round in a circle, pretending to look around him. 'Like you look for someone, or something?'

'No,' I said. I hadn't realized but I must have been looking for the Spook. 'Nothing,' I said. 'No one.'

He left me at our gate. I thought for a moment of inviting him in. But I didn't want him to meet Mum and Dad. It was too soon and they might be in a bad mood.

It was just as well I didn't. I knew something was wrong the moment I walked into the kitchen and they're both sitting there staring at me.

'What?' I said.

Dad holds up a newspaper. It was the *Evening Standard*.

'This,' he says.

There was this huge headline, spread across the top of the page:

Leo Lyall Joins Schoolgirls' Crusade
to Save the World

And a picture of me and Nina with Leo Lyall on Fort Doom.

'We've just had a call from the school,' Mum says. 'From the headteacher. He wants to talk to us. This evening.'

16

Banned

It must have been Ella – the press officer Tariq brought out with him in the helicopter. Or Mei.

I can remember both of them taking pictures when we were at the fort. But I didn't expect to see them splashed all over the *Evening Standard*.

And on top of that, there's all these quotes from me about how I'd got the idea from a history lesson about the Children's Crusade and how we're going to shame the older generation into taking action before it's too late.

'But I didn't know it was for the newspapers,' I said. 'I thought we were just discussing it – you know – between ourselves.'

No good. Dad's got this tight line where his mouth

should be and Mum's going, 'Oh, Kit.'

And I'm thinking, this has got nothing to do with the conference; it's because of Leo Lyall.

The headteacher was even worse. Mr Swanwick. Most of the kids in Year Seven called him Duckweed. I won't tell you what the rest of the school called him but it was worse.

We saw him in his office. Me and my mum and dad. He'd got a copy of the *Evening Standard* on his desk. The chairman of the school governors has been onto him, he says, and they are both very concerned.

'We have the good name of the school to consider,' he says.

'So why is that a problem?' says my dad.

I'll say this for my dad: whatever he thought about it himself, he wasn't going to have Old Duckweed having a go at me.

'I'd have thought the school would be only too pleased to be associated with a cause like this,' he told him in this lazy, bored voice he uses when he's dealing with what he calls Authority. My dad doesn't like Authority. I think it comes of being a photographer.

'I think we can confidently assume,' says Duckweed, 'that the only cause that interests this fellow is the sale of a few million more of his discs.'

Discs. It's sad really. And this man is the head of a school.

'And I fail to see how the school can possibly benefit from its association with an egotistical maniac whose only interest is in self-promotion.'

I gathered he meant Leo Lyall. He-Who-Cannot-Be-Named.

'I am afraid that these two young ladies . . .' – that's me and Nina – 'have been duped.'

He was prepared to take this into consideration, he said, when taking whatever action was necessary.

I was about to say something when Mum starts.

'Honestly, you'd think they were criminals,' she says indignantly. 'You should be proud that at least two pupils in your school care a bit more about the future of the world than they do about the football results.'

I looked at her in amazement. I don't know where she'd got that idea from, but it was nice to hear her sticking up for me for a change.

It didn't do any good though.

'I'm sorry,' says Duckweed, 'but the chairman of the school governors has made his views very clear and I am one hundred per cent behind him. A school of Waverley's reputation cannot be associated with a cheap publicity stunt orchestrated by a man whose own reputation, quite frankly, leaves a great deal to be desired. Moreover,' he went on when he saw she was about to interrupt, 'while I am firmly of the opinion that this whole idea is no more than a frivolous attempt to gain a few headlines – and that there is not the slightest chance of it going anywhere – I am seriously concerned that any future activities of this nature will seriously interfere with your daughter's education.'

That shut my mother up. I knew it would. He glanced down at a file he had in front of him. 'Catherine –' The way he said it I knew it was written down in front of him – 'Catherine is already involved in a large number of extra-curricular activities.' He read from the list. 'Football, rock climbing, swimming, kick-boxing . . .' He raised his eyebrows at the last one and shot me a look. 'If she insists on continuing with this, I am afraid you will have to remove her to another school where she can indulge in such distractions without fear of slipping behind in her academic work.'

'Absolute nonsense!' said Tariq when we went round there afterwards. 'Complete rubbish! Education has absolutely nothing to do with it. Do you know the real reason? It's because the chairman of the school governors is a reactionary old so-and-so who thinks climate change is something made up by people like me to line our own pockets. And do you know how he made his own money?'

We didn't.

'In the oil business,' he said. 'Persuading people to use up even more fossil fuel. I've had trouble with him before.'

'So we're going to fight it,' says Nina, eyes shining. She loves a fight.

But no. It turned out we weren't going to fight it.

'Let's face it, they hold all the cards,' said Tariq miserably. 'We don't want you both thrown out of school. And even if we appealed the decision, they could make life very difficult for you in other ways. No, I think we just have to take a hit on this one. Live to fight another day.'

I caught Nina's eye. She opened her mouth. Wait for it, I thought. But then her mouth snaps shut. She doesn't say a word.

She didn't say another word all the time we were there. Tariq is apologizing to Mum and Dad for getting us involved with Leo Lyall, and Nina is just sitting there taking it, quiet as a mouse. I couldn't believe it.

Maybe she's decided her father's right, I thought. It would be a first, but still . . .

I should have known better.

When I get home there's a note from her on Facebook. She'd sent it to everyone on the steering committee:

Emergency meeting – Saturday 11a.m. My place.

What's she up to? I wondered. I tried to talk to her about it at school the next day but she's still saying nothing. She was the same all day Friday, but I know Nina when she's like this. It means she's plotting something.

But even in my worst nightmares, I could never have imagined it would turn out the way it did. And to be fair, there's no way Nina could either.

17

Fireworks

So – Saturday morning I'm getting my bike out to cycle over to Nina's, and Mum's standing there blocking the door.

'Where do you think you're going?' she says.

'Nina's,' I said. 'I told you.'

'No, you didn't,' she says. (I did actually. She may have been on the phone at the time, but I did.) 'And don't say I never listen because I do and this is the first I've heard of it. Why are you going to Nina's?'

I'd told her that, too. 'To do my homework,' I said.

'Can't you do your homework by yourself? Why do you always have to do it at Nina's?'

There were several answers to this but I picked the

hardest one for her to argue with.

'We're working on a project. You have to do it together.'

'What project?'

'The bird life on the River Thames.'

I'm getting better at this; it worries me sometimes. I wondered if it was another sign of me turning into the Spook.

She muttered something under her breath.

'I'm sorry?' I said, raising my eyes the way she does when I mutter at her.

'I said, we've had a bit too much of you and Nina and your projects.'

'What's that supposed to mean?'

'Never mind. When will you be back?'

'About five?'

'All right, but no later than five, do you understand?'

Honestly, she's like my jailer or something. She's been like this since my dad came back and found out about Leo Lyall. The funny thing is she's been dead nice to him. But she makes up for it with the way she treats me. Maybe she just needs someone to get at all the time and now it's my turn.

And she hasn't finished with me yet.

'Have you got lipstick on?' she says, peering at me.

'No,' I said indignantly. 'Why would I wear lipstick to go to Nina's?'

I looked in the mirror in the hall. My lips did look quite red but it wasn't lipstick. I was going to put it on when I left the house. A touch of mascara, too, because Raoul's going to be there and I reckon Amor Gagalac's got her eye on him, and with a name like that you can't take any chances. I've got them in the pocket of my jacket with my make-up mirror. I was wearing the red leather jacket Dad brought back from his last trip to the States and my denim skinnies.

'Honestly,' I said, 'you'd think it was a police state or something.'

She's still looking at me all suspicious but then her expression changes.

'I'm sorry,' she says. 'I've been a bit hard on you lately, haven't I?'

And now I'm the one looking suspicious, because she always does this to me. If she can't get anywhere being strict she goes all soft on me and I weaken.

Not this time, though. I shrugged.

She opened her arms and gave me a hug and kissed the top of my head.

'Make sure you ride carefully,' she says. 'We might

go out to eat tonight. Just the three of us. Would you like that?'

'Yeah, that'd be great,' I said. I felt terrible.

I felt terrible all the way across the Common. It didn't stop me putting on lipstick and mascara, though. I did it just on the other side of the railway line. I didn't go over the top, just a hint of both. At one stage I thought I sensed the Spook watching me with her horrible smirk, but I looked round very carefully and I couldn't see any sign of her. It's like she's standing behind me all the time. Between her and my mother it feels like I'm always being watched, inside the house and out.

I get to Nina's. 'Have you got eye make-up on?' she says.

I don't believe this.

'Just a bit,' I said. 'I haven't been sleeping well.'

This was true.

'Hmmm,' she says. 'Well, they're all here. Except Raoul.'

Damn! They were sitting round the table in the kitchen. Nina had put juice and biscuits out. She seemed a bit nervous.

'Where's your mum and dad?' I said.

'Gone shopping,' she says. 'Omar's looking after

me.' She rolled her eyes.

I didn't need to ask where Omar was, at 11 o'clock on Saturday morning.

'We'll give Raoul five more minutes,' says Nina, 'and then we'll start.'

The minutes ticked by. Still no Raoul. Nina's looking at the kitchen clock all the time. I don't think I'd ever seen her this nervous.

'OK,' she says, when the clock's on five past. 'We'd better start . . .' But she's glancing anxiously towards the window. I wondered if she was desperate for Raoul to be there, too. There'd been no sign of it so far but you never know with Nina. 'Well, you all know what's happened,' she said. 'So I've called this meeting to discuss what we can do about it.'

'What *can* we do about it?' said Li Ching. 'We don't want to be chucked out of school.'

'No one's going to chuck us out of school,' said Nina. 'Not if we play our cards right. They wouldn't dare. It's all bluff.'

The doorbell rang and she practically jumped out of her chair and ran to the window. But she looked disappointed. 'It's only Raoul,' she said.

I tried to look as if I couldn't care less.

'Who else were you expecting?' I said.

But she was already on her way to the door. They came back in together but she's nagging him for being late. His eyes are roaming across the table. Blush, I told myself, and you're dead. Then his eyes met mine and I didn't think about anything else for a while.

In fact it was a few minutes before I started listening to what Nina was saying.

'Blah di blah di blah . . . and so I sent this email to Leo Lyall.'

There's a stunned silence. I was the first to find my voice.

'You did *what?*' I said.

'I thought I'd let him know what was going on,' she said. 'It's only fair – he is our major sponsor.'

'Does your dad know?' I said.

'What's it got to do with my dad?' she says. 'This is a children's conference – or have you forgotten?'

As if Leo Lyall wasn't an adult. Well, maybe she's right about that.

'You mean *the* Leo Lyall?' says Lucy.

'We told you we'd met him,' says Nina.

'Yes, but . . .' Lucy's eyes slide round the table. 'We didn't think . . . I mean . . .'

What she meant was she hadn't believed us, and I don't blame her.

'And I suppose he wrote back?' says Li Ching. Ha ha.

'Yes,' says Nina. 'As a matter of fact he did. Personally.'

They didn't really believe her but she seemed so sure of herself.

'And?' I said.

'He said he's one hundred per cent behind us – and he'd try and drop round.'

'Drop round?' This is Lucy, but they're all staring at Nina now. 'You mean here? Now?'

'That's what he said.'

I didn't believe this for a minute, but I was more interested in the first bit. 'What do you mean, one hundred per cent behind us?' I said. 'One hundred per cent behind what?'

'Whatever we decide we're going to do about this,' said Nina. 'Look.' She stares round the table. 'Do we want this conference to go ahead or don't we?'

'Well, yes,' I said, 'but . . .'

'So the first thing we have to do is publicize it,' she says. 'If we get the media behind us, they won't be able to do anything to stop us.'

'It was because of the media that we got banned in the first place,' I pointed out. 'If that story hadn't been in the *Standard* . . .'

'I mean the social media,' said Nina. 'What we need is a worldwide protest. Think of the publicity for the conference. Do you know how many followers Leo Lyall's got on Twitter? Over two million. Get them behind us and Old Duckweed won't be able to do a thing about it.'

They were looking doubtful.

'So when do you expect Leo Lyall to drop by?' says Li, still being sarcastic.

Nina stands up and crosses over to the window. 'This'll be him now,' she says.

A stretch limo had just pulled up outside the house.

We watched in amazement as the driver stepped out onto the pavement and opened the back door. A tall figure stepped out, dressed all in black. Black leather jacket, shiny black skinnies, black high-heeled boots.

It was Mei.

Nina goes out to meet her. We're all watching from the window.

'Do you think Leo Lyall's in the car?' says Nicky.

After a short conversation Nina comes back inside.

She still looked confident, but there was a slight edge of uncertainty about her. Perhaps it was only me who noticed.

'He's got held up,' she said.

'Oh yeah,' said Li.

'He's in the recording studio,' said Nina, 'but he wants us to go there to meet him.'

We all look at each other.

'Now?'

'Now,' says Nina.

'In that?' says Amor.

'Of course in that. That's what he's sent it for.'

'I've never been in a stretch limo,' says Amor.

None of us had.

'Let's put it to the vote,' says Nina. 'All those in favour.'

She put her hand up. I felt everyone was looking at me.

What could I do? I know you should never get in a car with a stranger, not unless you're with someone like your parents or a teacher. But Mei wasn't really a stranger and there were seven of us. And there were other considerations. The conference had been my idea in the first place. I didn't want Nina to think I was ready to give up the first time we hit a problem. And I didn't want Raoul to think it either.

I put up my hand.

Raoul said later he only voted for it because I had. And Li said he only voted for it because Raoul had. So you could say it was my fault.

'Great,' says Nina. 'That's four. Come on, let's make it unanimous.'

So in the end all seven of us pile in the limo. We were quite excited now. I looked back as we set off, and Omar's standing at the window in his dressing gown staring out at us. It was worth it just to see the expression on his face.

So we're all lounging about in this stretch limo driving along the South Circular, listening to Zeitgeist on the speakers and drinking fruit juice – pomegranate juice, in fact, which was all there was, Mei said, apart from booze.

'I don't mind booze,' said Amor Gagalac. Mei smiled as if it was a joke.

'Where's this studio?' I said.

'You know,' said Mei. 'You've been there before.'

'You don't mean the fort?' I said.

'Of course,' she said. 'Where else?'

I suppose I should have thought of that, but really,

it just hadn't occurred to me.

There was a boat waiting for us at Greenwich. An RHIB with an outboard. We all had to put lifejackets on.

'I don't know about this,' said Nicky, who was starting to look worried. 'How far are we going?'

'You'll be there and back in an hour,' said Mei. 'This thing doesn't hang about.'

She wasn't joking. It was almost as fast as the helicopter, but nothing like as smooth. We're all hanging on for dear life and you could hardly see a thing for spray. It was only when we were out in the river that I realized Mei wasn't with us.

It was a great ride though, once you got used to bouncing on water. We were through the Thames Barrier within about five minutes of leaving Greenwich and the next landmark I saw was the Queen Elizabeth Bridge, hundreds of feet above the river between Kent and Essex. Then we were heading out into the Thames Estuary.

The sea was quite calm but there was a haze of autumn mist in the air and the seven towers looked even weirder than the first time we'd seen them. There was a bit of a subdued atmosphere now. Lucy and Amor were feeling sick and Nicky said she'd told her mum she'd be back for lunch. She texted her but she didn't want to tell her where she really was. She just said the meeting was running on a bit and she'd be later than she said.

I was more than a bit worried myself. If my parents knew what I was doing they'd go completely mental. I couldn't believe I'd gone along with Nina now.

'How long are we going to be out here?' I said to her.

'Oh about half an hour should be enough,' she said. 'Don't worry, we'll easily be back for five. They'll never know you've been out of Balham.'

That wasn't really the point, though. It may not seem like it, but I wasn't in the habit of going completely against their wishes. And yet a part of me was thinking they should have been straight with me and told me exactly why they didn't want me having anything to do with Leo Lyall.

We slowed right down and cruised into the docking area under the first tower. One of the crew helped us onto the ladder and we climbed up into the reception area. It was exactly the same as the first time me and Nina had been here. The magic piano playing its ghostly music and the robot dancers going round and round on the dance floor. The others were just staring around as if they'd landed on Mars. And in a way they had.

Then a voice I recognize from before says: 'Welcome to Fort Doom. Kindly follow the signs until you reach the Residential Tower.'

Hal. The speaking computer.

We looked for the signs and there's a red light flashing above the door. It opened automatically as we walked towards it and then we're out on the catwalks.

Even though I'd been here before I was feeling quite nervous and it must have been much worse for the others – especially when we saw the boat heading back towards London in a cloud of spray.

'Why's it leaving?' says Nicky. Her voice was like a wail. 'What's going on?'

'It's probably just gone to fetch something from the shore,' said Nina. 'It'll be straight back.'

She sounded calm enough but I knew she had no idea.

'I'm phoning Mum,' said Nicky.

'Just wait till we get to the next tower,' Nina told her. 'We don't want to hang around on the catwalk.'

She was right about that. There was a chill in the air and the mist seemed to be thickening. We hurried on until we saw another flashing light ahead of us and a door slid open. We stepped through.

'Oh my god,' says Lucy. 'It's Dracula's castle.'

I knew what she meant. This was the Great Hall where we'd had tea. But there was no tea now. Just the suits of armour and the demons huddled round the fireplace. We were in a bit of a huddle ourselves, like scared little mice waiting for the cat to pounce.

'Hi,' says a voice from above. 'Welcome to Fort Doom.'

Different voice from last time. We all looked up – and there's Leo Lyall standing on the minstrels' gallery.

Then this music starts. It was like a fanfare of trumpets. But after a few seconds I realized it was from 'Requiem for a Dying Planet'. It's blaring out of hidden speakers, filling the whole room. And there's smoke swirling around and lights are flashing on and off in different colours from red to blue to green, like in a disco. You can hardly make out what's happening but the suits of armour are jerking about as if they're dancing and Leo comes swinging down from the minstrels' gallery on a rope and lands right in the middle of the hall.

Leo likes to make an entrance, I remembered Mei

saying the last time we were here. I wished she was here now. I felt she was a kind of restraining influence. Without her, you never knew what Leo might do.

He was wearing some kind of tunic in lots of different colours, like a patchwork quilt. With pink-and-white striped trousers tucked into red boots. We were all standing there, still looking like scared mice, but he strides up to us and he's shaking hands with everyone and going, 'Hello, I'm Leo Lyall,' as if we don't know, and Nina's doing her best to introduce us all.

Then I find myself staring into his eyes. They're almost hypnotic, especially in this light.

'We need no introduction,' he says. 'How are you, Catherine?' Then he peers at me a bit more sternly. 'Are you wearing eye make-up?' he says.

Honestly, he's as bad as Mum.

But then he says, 'I must show you how to put it on properly.'

And I realize, of course, that he's wearing it too.

Then before I can say anything the music fades and a voice says, 'We have visitors.'

Hal again.

Leo raises his own voice. 'OK,' he says. 'Thank you, Hal. Let's have some light on the scene.'

One of the tapestries rolled back like a curtain and we're gazing through this huge glass panel – you could hardly call it a window – with a panoramic view of the whole estuary. It was like a painting. Except there was movement on it. Coming towards us, flying low across the water, was a helicopter.

You could hear it. Much louder than it should have been at this distance. Like a lawnmower mowing the sky. It took me a moment to realize the sound was being relayed through the speakers. It was like part of the music. All those weird chords and vocals and the sound of the helicopter.

'I love the smell of napalm in the morning,' says Leo in this fake American accent.

We all looked at him. What was he on about?

'Apocalypse Now,' he says. 'Have you seen the movie?' He looks at us and grins. I think that's when I realized it wasn't just an act, him being mad. He really was. Mad as a box of frogs. 'I guess it's a bit before your time,' he said.

'I have,' says Li. But he's watching the helicopter and frowning.

'Is this coming for us?' says Nicky. She's probably still worried about getting home for lunch.

'I very much think so,' says Leo.

It was then that we saw the markings.

'It's the police,' said Li.

'But – why?' I said.

'Because I sent for them, Princess.' This is Leo. 'We need an audience. Without an audience you are nothing. Isn't that right, Hal?'

'If you say so,' said the voice, gloomily.

The helicopter was almost hovering above the landing tower. 'Very well,' said Leo. He was shouting now above the noise of the helicopter and the music. 'Let the wild rumpus begin.'

18

The Pied Piper

There was a brilliant flash of light and a huge explosion. The landing tower vanished in a ball of yellow-orange fire that seemed to flatten and spread sideways over the sea like a pancake. We all hit the floor as soon as it happened but we could feel our own tower tremble from the blast. When we climbed to our feet and looked out of the window again, there was just this great black cloud of smoke where the landing tower had been.

There was no sign of the helicopter, but then we saw it emerge from the top of the smoke, much higher than before. It had given up the idea of landing though. There was nothing left to land on. What was left of the tower had collapsed into the sea. After buzzing about for a minute or two like an angry wasp, the helicopter turned and headed back for the shore.

'Thank you, Hal,' said Leo. 'Very neatly done if I may say so.'

'Don't mention it,' said the voice, in the same sardonic tone as when he'd thanked it for arranging tea.

We were just standing there, shocked. Then there's this strange sound. It's Nicky. She's got both hands over her mouth and there's these noises coming from her, like a kind of whooping, rising and falling as if she's struggling for breath. Lucy put her arm round her until she'd calmed down a bit and started to sob.

'OK,' said Leo, 'let's go down into the playroom.'

None of us moved. We're still staring at the black smoke, drifting slowly away over the sea, and the three broken legs of the tower sticking up out of the water and the wreckage floating on the waves, and the distant helicopter vanishing into the mist.

'Come on,' Leo says impatiently. 'I've got a new game we can play.'

I came to my senses. I walked up to him. 'What do you think you're doing?' I said. My voice sounded quite calm really. I don't know how I managed that. Inside I was in a state of complete panic.

'What's the matter, Principessa?' He looked puzzled.

'What's the matter?' I said. 'You've just blown up the landing pad. You almost blew a police helicopter out of the sky. You're asking me what's the matter?'

'Well, it was your idea,' he said.

'*My* idea? It was *not* my idea,' I said. I was sounding like Mum. 'How was it my idea?'

'OK. But it was you who put the idea into my head. You know? The Pied Piper of Hamelin?'

'*What?*' I said. 'What's the Pied Piper got to do with anything?'

But I had a horrible idea that I knew. That was why he was wearing this ridiculous jacket.

'The Pied Piper and the children of Hamelin,' he says. 'When the mayor and the corporation tried to muck him about.'

'OK,' I said. I knew I was dealing with a madman so I kept my voice calm. 'You're not the Pied Piper of Hamelin and we're not the children of Hamelin.'

'If you say so, Principessa,' he said. 'But I think they'll get the message.'

'What message?' said Nina, who'd found her voice at last.

'That unless they play ball, they'll never see their children again.'

That started Nicky off again. I can't say I blamed her, but I wished she'd shut up. It was bad enough with 'Requiem for a Dying Planet' blaring out of the speakers. I could hardly hear myself think.

'Right, listen up,' said Leo, raising his hands as if he's trying to calm down an angry mob. 'You're not going to come to any harm, I promise you. But they don't know that. They're going to think I've finally flipped.'

No, I thought. How could they possibly think that?

'So what do you think they're going to do about it?' I said.

'Well, the next thing is they're going to send the Mayor of London to negotiate with me.'

'Boris Johnson?' says Nina, as if this is the looniest idea yet, even more loony than nearly blowing up a police helicopter.

'That's your man,' he says. 'Unless they've elected a new mayor. Have they?'

Nina shook her head.

'So – what makes you think Boris Johnson's going to come here?' I said, humouring him.

'Because I've just tweeted him,' said Leo. 'I've said that unless he comes here by six o' clock I'm going to blow us all up.'

'Will somebody shut that girl up,' said Nina, putting her hands over her ears as Nicky started howling again. Amor Gagalac had joined her.

'How are you going to do that?' I asked Leo. Again, I had a horrible feeling I knew.

'Same as I blew the last tower up,' he said. 'I've got every single tower rigged with explosives and I'm going to blow them up one by one until they agree to our terms.'

'*Our* terms?' I said.

'That's right,' he says. 'We're all in this together.'

'And what terms are these?'

He ticked them off on his fingers. 'A – the school withdraws its objections to the children's conference. B – delegates are flown in free from all over the world at the expense of the City of London. And C . . .' he frowned. 'I've forgotten what C is. What was C?'

I wondered if he was on something. Stupid of me, really. Of course he was. Not that he really needed anything. He was hooked on something stronger than any drug. He was hooked on Leo Lyall.

'Oh, I know,' he said. 'The Royal Albert Hall.'

'What do you want with the Royal Albert Hall?' I said.

'I don't want it. Been there, done that. It's for you, Princess, for your conference.'

He beamed at me as if he'd done the whole thing just for me. And maybe he had.

'And what do you think they'll give you?' I said. 'Apart from twenty years?'

'Twenty years?' he said, looking puzzled. 'Why would they give me twenty years?'

'Look what you just did.' I pointed out the window. The cloud was still drifting away over the water and there were three shattered stumps sticking up where the tower had stood.

'It was my tower,' he said sulkily. 'I could do what I liked with it.'

'And what about us?' I said.

'What about you?'

'You've just kidnapped seven children,' I pointed out. 'You'll get *at least* twenty years for that.'

'Who says I kidnapped you?' he said. 'You've just come to play games. Come on now, down to the playroom.'

What more could you say? We followed him down to the playroom.

19

The Siege of Fort Doom

We watched the sun setting over the water. It was a very deep, dark red and it made the water the colour of blood.

There were about a dozen boats out there. Mostly police launches, but a couple of others that looked like they might be Royal Navy patrol boats. Above them there were three circling helicopters and a light aircraft, but they kept to a safe distance. I wondered if the Mayor of London was out there.

Leo had left us in the playroom. Not that any of us felt like playing. We were just standing by the windows, staring out at the rescue fleet. So near but so far. We couldn't even talk to them. Leo had made us give him all our phones.

'So they don't try and talk you into doing something stupid,' he said.

He said he'd do all the negotiating for us. We just had to trust him. We didn't find this reassuring.

There were plenty of computers around but the Internet had been blocked. I suppose that was Hal. Leo said Hal was in control of the explosives, too. If anything happened to him, he said, Hal would look after us. We didn't find this reassuring either. There was a CCTV camera high on the wall – like one of Hal's eyes watching us.

Raoul had found a camcorder among all the toys and things and he was busy filming the scene outside before we lost the light. He was the only one of us who seemed quite cheerful. He'd always wanted to film a running news story, he said.

'Just a pity we're in it,' I told him.

I was thinking about my parents watching all this on TV. They'd been right about Leo. But why was he doing all this? It couldn't just be for us.

'I knew he was mad,' said Nina quietly in my ear, as if she'd been mind-reading. 'But I didn't know he was this mad.'

'What do you think they'll do?' I said, meaning the people in the boats.

'They'll negotiate,' said Nina. 'They always do.'

'They could promise anything,' I said. 'It doesn't mean it'll happen, once he lets us go.'

'I know,' she said. 'That's why he can't let us go.'

We were keeping our voices down. We didn't want the others to hear, quite apart from Leo or his friend Hal.

'He can't keep us here for ever,' I said. 'He's got to let some of us go to organize the conference.'

'He's probably thought of that,' she said. 'He's probably going to let one or two of us go and keep the rest here as hostages. Or else . . .' Her voice trailed off.

'What?' I said.

'Maybe he'll just keep you.'

'Why me?'

'I don't know.' She shrugged. 'But it's like he's got a *thing* about you. Like he's trying to impress you or something. All this Princess stuff. Maybe you should try and reason with him.'

'Me?' I glared at her. 'Why not you? You sent him the email.'

A panel slid back in the ceiling above us and Leo peered down at us.

'Principessa,' he says.

'That's you,' said Nina.

'Can you come up here a minute?' he says.

I went up the spiral staircase into the Great Hall. He was sitting at the table with a laptop.

'Come and sit here,' he says.

I sat next to him. Boris Johnson was on the screen. He was on Skype.

'This is Kit,' says Leo.

'Hello, Kit,' says Boris. 'How you keeping?'

'Fine, thank you,' I said.

I can't believe it. I'm speaking to the Mayor of London on Skype. I'm being held hostage by a mad rock singer on a fort in the middle of the Thames Estuary and I'm saying: 'Fine, thank you,' to the Mayor of London.

'You being treated all right?' says Boris.

'Not too bad,' I said.

'And how are the other kids?'

'They're OK. I mean, they'd rather be back home, but apart from that, you know . . .'

'I know,' he said. 'We're doing all we can, I promise you. We want all this to end peacefully, don't we, Leo?'

'That's up to you,' said Leo, sitting next to me.

'Now, Kit,' says Boris. 'I believe this conference was your idea.'

'Yes,' I said, 'but I never meant it to be like this.'

'We know that,' he said. 'But what exactly did you have in mind?'

'Tell him you want the Royal Albert Hall,' said Leo.

'I never said anything about the Albert Hall,' I said to him. 'I don't care where we meet.'

'That's very reasonable,' said Boris.

'Hang on, hang on,' said Leo. 'You don't wriggle out of it that easy.'

'I'm not trying to wriggle out of anything,' said the mayor. 'I haven't agreed anything. I told you, I am not prepared to negotiate with terrorists.'

Leo said something rude. 'Can you believe this?' he says to me.

'All I will promise,' said Boris, 'is that if this young lady wishes to discuss the matter with me in the proper manner and the school authorities are in agreement . . .' he paused.

'Go on,' said Leo, 'you'll do what?'

'I will see if there is anything I can do to facilitate the proposal. But only if you are prepared to release the hostages and give yourself up to the police.'

'Nothing doing,' said Leo. 'I want a firmer commitment than that. I know you politicians with your weasel words. Go facilitate yourself. Over and out.'

He clicked on the mouse and Boris disappeared.

'Bloody politicians,' Leo said.

'I never said I wanted the Albert Hall,' I said. 'That was you.'

'Oh shut up,' he said. 'You try to do your best for people . . .'

'This is your best?' I waved towards the window. It was growing dark and the boats had their lights on. 'We're surrounded by armed police. You've got the place rigged up with explosives. You call the Mayor of London a – well, what you called him. If this is your best, I'd hate to see your worst.'

'I'm only doing it for you,' he said sulkily.

'For me? If you want to do something for me, you can start by letting us all go home.'

'I can't do that,' he said.

'Well, what about if I stay and the rest of them go?'

He looked at me. 'Would you do that?'

I nodded.

'Well, I'll think about it,' he said. 'Let's just give

Boris and his mates a bit longer to sweat it out. They might come round.'

'Where we going to spend the night?' I said. 'Down there?'

'There's nothing wrong with it, is there? You've got plenty to do.'

'There's no beds.'

'I'll get mattresses.'

'And what about something to eat?'

'I'll see to that. Are you hungry?'

'I haven't eaten since breakfast. Of course I'm hungry.'

'Sorry.' He looked crestfallen. 'Not much of a father, am I?'

I stared at him. 'What are you talking about? You're not my father.'

'Oh yes, I am,' he said quietly.

I shook my head. 'You're mad,' I said. But I was all twisted up inside. Now we were getting down to it and I wasn't at all sure I wanted to.

'You ask your mother,' he said.

'I wish I could,' I muttered. I could feel the tears coming then but I rubbed at my cheeks angrily.

'There's no need to cry,' he said. 'It's me who should be crying. Believe me, I've wept buckets. For you *and* your mother.'

I really didn't want to hear this. Not now.

I stood up. 'I want to join the others,' I said.

He looked up at me, smiling sadly. 'Don't worry,' he said. 'I won't be here much longer.'

'What? Where are you going to go?'

'I'm dying,' he said.

I didn't know if I'd heard him properly. His voice was so matter-of-fact. It was like he'd said, I'm thirsty.

'I've got six months to live,' he said. 'At the most.'

'Don't be stupid,' I said, when I found my voice. 'You look fine. What's wrong with you?'

'That doesn't matter.' He shrugged. 'All that matters is that I do something right for a change.'

'Something right?' I stared at him. 'You think this is doing something right?'

'I think so,' he said. 'And you'll think so too, when you're a bit older.'

I felt like hitting him. I couldn't believe he was dying, but even if he was, this was just . . . I knew what Mum would call it cos she says it about anyone who cries when they want something. She says it's emotional blackmail.

'If you have got something wrong with you, you need help,' I said.

248

'I've had help,' he told me. 'I've had all the help they can give me. Substance abuse, that's what they call it. My liver can't take it any more.'

'Then stop taking drugs,' I said.

'Too late for that. We are what we are.'

'For heaven's sake . . .' I turned away from him and brushed at the tears. Tears of anger this time.

'Don't cry for me,' he said.

'I wasn't,' I said.

'OK.' His voice was harder. 'Go and join the others. I'll be down in a few minutes. With some food. At least I can do that much.'

I went down the stairs. Nina and Raoul were waiting for me at the bottom.

'What's up?' said Nina when she saw my face. 'We were just going to come up for you'

'Did he do anything . . . ?' Raoul was glaring up the stairs.

'No,' I said. 'It's all right.'

I started to tell them what had happened – the bit about the mayor anyway – but then Li called out from one of the windows.

'There's a boat coming,' he said.

We joined him at the window. We could just see the lights of the boat and the small bow wave but it was definitely coming towards us. It was about a hundred metres from where the reception tower had been.

'Maybe it's the SAS,' said Li.

Suddenly a bright light came on. A searchlight, high up in one of the towers. We could see the boat clearly now. It was a small open boat with an outboard and there was only one person in it.

It was my mother.

20

Skeletons in the Cupboard

The boat came closer and closer and then turned under the tower with the searchlight on it and vanished into the darkness.

I went up the stairs but the door at the top was locked. I hammered on it and shouted until Nina made me come down.

'Are you *sure* it was your mother?' Li said.

'Pretty sure,' I said.

'But what can *she* do?'

'Talk to him. Try to reason with him.'

'But why would he listen to *her*?' Lucy wanted to know.

I just shrugged and said I didn't know. I was trying to make sense of it myself – and the things Leo had told me.

Raoul was still messing about with the camera. He was beginning to annoy me. As if it mattered. I didn't want to be recorded for posterity; I just wanted to get out alive. And I was worried sick about my mother.

We waited down there for about an hour. No one wanted to play with Leo's toys. We just sat around or paced about or gazed out the window at the little fleet of boats. They didn't seem to be doing much. Probably they were just waiting, too.

Then suddenly we heard the door open at the top of the stairs and Mum was there. I ran up to her and we met about halfway. She wrapped her arms around me. The door closed.

The others were waiting for us in a huddle at the bottom of the stairs. Mum went straight over to Nina and gave her a hug.

'Your mum and dad send their love,' she said. 'And Omar says hang on in there.'

'Yeah, great,' says Nina. 'Thanks, Omar. So what's happening?'

Mum sighed. 'Nothing, I'm afraid. Leo's still waiting to hear from the authorities.'

'But what does he want? Does he want a ransom or something?'

'I don't think he knows what he wants. He never has.'

'So what do we do now?' Li asked.

'I'm afraid we wait,' she said. 'Until they sort something out.'

'So you're a hostage, too?' I said.

She managed to smile. 'Looks like it.'

'But why did they let you come?' Nina demanded. 'By yourself without any back up?' Nina watches a lot of detective series.

'They thought I might be able to reason with him,' she said.

I could see Nina was still puzzled. They all were. Why send *her*? But whatever it was she wasn't prepared to tell them, and after a while most people drifted back to the windows or poked around looking for a way out. I was pretty sure there wasn't one, or we'd have found it already. The only way out was up the stairs to the Great Hall where Leo was – and he'd locked the door.

After a while Mum caught my eye and we walked over to one of the windows at the far end of the room where we could talk quietly by ourselves.

'So what's Leo been saying to you?' she said.

'He said he was my father,' I said. I could hardly bring myself to look at her.

'And you believed him?'

'Why would he say it, if it wasn't true?'

'Because – oh, honestly Kit . . .'

'I don't know what to believe,' I said.

'You don't even look like him. You look exactly like your dad. I mean, your *real* dad. Even you must be able to see that. You're a lot prettier, of course,' she said hastily, 'but you've got the same hair, the same eyes, the same shape face . . . Come here.' She drew me to her and buried her face in my hair. 'Leo Lyall is not your father,' she said softly. 'And I ought to know.'

I think I felt relieved. But it's hard to know exactly what I felt. I think it was mainly confused.

'I don't understand,' I muttered.

'All right.' I felt her sigh. 'I suppose I owe you an explanation. But look –' She leant back and took hold of my chin to turn my face up to her – 'this is not something I'm proud of, right? And it's not something I'm that happy about sharing with you – or anyone for that matter. There are some things you just don't share with people, least of all your own daughter.'

I braced myself.

'OK. I knew Leo when I was at uni. When I was

a swimmer. I wasn't really famous but . . . there was a lot of stuff on the news about the Olympics and I was one of the young hopefuls in those days so . . . To cut a long story short, we went out together. For about a year. Then we split up. He was a crazy man, even then. But, you know, it was kind of fun, in some ways. I was only twenty-two. A lot of things seemed fun then that would be . . . not so much fun now. But even then I knew I didn't want that kind of life. I mean, I didn't really know what I wanted but it wasn't that. Then, some years later, I met your dad. And I knew – this was it. He was the one for me. I'm sorry – I'm embarrassing you, but it's true.'

'I'm not embarrassed,' I said, even though I was a bit.

'Well, the trouble was, we'd only been going out a few months when I had my accident. And I had to give up being a swimmer. Your dad was so nice about it. So supportive. And we got married but – but somehow, something inside me . . . I don't know, I thought it was like he was just sorry for me. And then, you know, Mum got ill. I tried to do what I could, to be there for her, but – she just . . . She was always so . . . and the drink didn't help.'

'The drink?'

'Yes, she was drinking quite a bit. I could understand why but . . . it was very difficult. And then, when she died . . .'

She was talking to me as if I knew all about it.

'It just broke me up. I was all over the place. Then there was the inquest, and they said how lonely she was – I just – I just wanted to be – I just wanted to get away. So I went away.' She took a deep breath. 'I went to New York. And I met Leo again.' She frowned. 'Do I really have to tell you all this?'

I nodded, but to be perfectly honest I wasn't sure I wanted to hear it.

'Well, we – we kind of got together again and . . .'

'Even though you were married to Dad.'

My voice sounded so hard I hardly recognized it.

'Oh god.' She leant her head against the window. 'I knew this was going to be difficult. You're only eleven years old. There's no way you can possibly understand this.' She was right there. 'I don't understand it myself. But – OK, it happened. I can't get round that. And then, I kind of . . . I realized what I was losing and . . . who I really *was*. And

I just— I told him it was no good. It wouldn't work. I loved your father and I certainly wasn't going to leave him for Leo Lyall.'

Mum dumped Leo Lyall. Can you believe this? Twice.

'So you went back to Dad?'

'Yes.'

'And did you tell him? Dad, I mean. About what had happened?'

'No.' She sighed. 'Not then. We decided to have a baby. I mean, I wanted to have a baby and . . .' She looked at me. 'I was so happy, and so was he; I didn't want to— and then Leo turns up.'

'And he thought I was his?'

'He just wouldn't accept that it had nothing to do with him. Or that I was finished with him for good. He's that kind of man. Everything has to revolve around him, you have no idea . . .' I think I probably could. 'I had to get a court order to make him leave us alone. And of course then I *had* to tell your father.' She looked so desolate I forgot how angry I was with her and nearly burst into tears and threw my arms round her. Somehow I managed to speak.

'Is that why you and Dad are – you know?' I didn't have to spell it out.

She nodded. 'I'm so sorry,' she said.

'But I'm not that man's daughter?' I felt I had to really get this straight.

'Kit, how many times do I have to tell you?'

'I just can't understand why he— why he's so sure about it.'

'With the kind of junk Leo's got swirling around in his head, I'd be surprised he knows what planet he's on half the time.'

There was a sudden commotion from the far side of the room. Nina and Amor were screaming at each other.

'Hey, you guys, break it up!' Mum went over to sort them out and I wandered off by myself to think about it.

And then I saw the Spook.

21

Apocalypse Now

She was standing next to the fantasy castle at the far end of the room. It was quite gloomy and I thought it was a trick of the light at first, or one of Leo's fantasy warriors. But then I went a bit closer. It was her all right. She was in her emo gear and she was looking at me in the way she has, like she cannot believe there are people this stupid in the world.

Then she turned around and walked straight through the wall.

I looked round to see if anyone else had seen it, but they'd all gathered round Nina and Amor, like when two kids are facing up to each other in the playground and everyone's hoping there's going to be a fight. They'd all be chanting, 'Fight, fight,' soon.

I looked back.

No sign of her. She'd walked right through the wall of the fantasy castle. Or else I was imagining it, and she hadn't been there in the first place. How could she have been there? We were on a fort in the middle of the Thames Estuary. I must be seeing things.

I walked a bit closer. Then she's there again, staring at me in complete amazement and shaking her head, like she cannot believe how stupid I am.

Then she turns round and walks through the wall again.

I looked back at the others but they're still arguing. I walked even closer. Then I went right up to the wall. I thought maybe there's a hidden door and I just can't see it. But there was nothing. I felt all over with my hands. It was painted to look like stone, but it was just wood. Even so, it was solid enough, and it was about two metres high.

I felt all the way to the end and then I peered round the corner of the turret – and there *was* a door. Or more a hatch, really. Like a cat flap. Or maybe a bit bigger than that – a dog flap. But it was made to look like a door. A castle door, like a kind of grating. A portcullis, I think it's called.

I got down on my hands and knees and peered through the grating. I felt like Alice in Wonderland when she's at the bottom of the rabbit hole. There was a dark tunnel on the other side but I could see light at the end of it. I tried to push the door open but it wouldn't move. Then I heard this voice in my head.

'Lift it, you Muppet.'

I stuck my finger in one of the holes near the bottom and lifted. Up it came. When it reached the top there was a click and it stayed there. The gap was plenty big enough for me to crawl through but I wasn't sure I wanted to.

I looked back to where the others were. Amor had started to cry now and Mum had her arm around her and Nina was picking a fight with someone else.

I stuck my head into the tunnel.

'Hello?' I said.

Nothing. Just a bit of an echo. Or else it was her saying Hello back. It sounded mocking.

I began to crawl through the tunnel. I was dead scared. I didn't know what I'd find at the other end. It's bad enough seeing a ghost standing outside your house under a street lamp but you don't want to find one at the end of a tunnel, especially not if you're crawling and you can't turn round and run screaming back the way you came.

The tunnel led to a kind of courtyard right in the middle of the castle. It was about two metres square, open at the top, with the walls and turrets of the castle all around – and all these fantasy figures on them, with their ugly scowling faces glaring down at me, waving swords and spears and battleaxes.

But no Spook.

I stood up. I really did feel like Alice then. When she nibbles the cake and gets bigger and bigger until she's nine feet tall. Then I felt really panicky 'cos I thought I might never be able to get out. I'd been lured into this strange fantasy world and I'd never be able to get back to the real one. I'd be a prisoner for ever with all these weirdos staring down at me.

But I could still hear my mum's voice – and Nina's. Quite distant, but obviously in the same world that I was in.

I dropped down on my hands and knees again to crawl back through the tunnel. And then I saw the trapdoor.

Actually, I felt it first.

It was set into the stone floor. Not that it *was* stone – it was wood, painted to look like stone, like the walls. But you could just see the line where the edge was. Then I saw the ring. A metal ring, set into the wood. I lifted it up and pulled. It wouldn't budge. I knelt up and braced myself and pulled again with all my strength but it was either locked or stuck solid.

Then suddenly I saw the boots.

Big black leather buckle boots with a skull on them.

I looked up. And there she was, staring down at me.

'You really are – the dumbest chick – I have ever met,' she says, in this flat, weary voice. 'And believe me I have met some dumb chicks.'

'What?' I said.

'You're kneeling on it,' she said. 'Dimwit.'

Well, she didn't say dim – I can't tell you what she really said – but that's what she meant.

I scrambled back off the trapdoor and pulled at the ring again. This time it came up easily.

'Thank you,' I said.

She shook her head, sighed, and walked back through the wall.

I peered down through the open trap. I could feel cold air on my face and smell the sea. I could hear it, too, sloshing around beneath me. But I couldn't see it. It was too dark. All I could see was the top of a metal ladder vanishing into space.

Then I heard Mum shouting for me.

I lowered the door and crawled back through the tunnel.

They'd suddenly realized I wasn't there and they were all looking for me.

'Over here!' I yelled. 'I've found the way—'

Then I clapped my hand over my mouth. I didn't want to let Hal know. I could see the CCTV camera at the far end of the room. His cold eye watching us. But it was quite dark where the castle was and the portcullis was on the other side from the camera.

They'd all gathered round. Mum looks up at the castle.

'Incredible,' she says. 'I suppose this is his Wendy House, is it? Where he plays with his dolls.'

'Actually it's a castle,' Li told her. He tended to take things a bit literally at times. 'It's for playing war games.'

I put my hand to my lips to warn them. Then I took Mum's arm and led her round the side and pointed. The rest of them all followed.

'It leads into a little courtyard,' I said quietly. 'And there's a trapdoor leading down to the sea.'

'I knew there had to be another way out,' Li said, smugly. 'For reasons of health and safety.'

I nearly kicked him. Personally I didn't think Leo Lyall would be too worried about health and safety.

Mum lay face down on the floor and started to wriggle through the tunnel, using her elbows to lever herself along. I followed – and Raoul and Li followed me.

I made them all stand close to the walls and pulled the trapdoor open.

They all peered down.

'You can't see anything,' I said. 'But I think it's water.'

Li looks at me. 'What else would it be?' he said.

He was almost as bad as the Spook.

Mum reached up and took down one of the Warhammer warriors from the battlements. A nasty-looking troll. Then she dropped it down the hole. We couldn't hear the splash, but I didn't know if this was because it was such a long way down or because of the sound of waves.

'Wait a minute,' says Li.

He wriggles back through the tunnel and comes back a few minutes later with one of Leo's model racing cars.

'Just what we need,' I said. 'A toy Ferrari.'

But he pressed a switch and the headlights came on. He gave me a smug look and pointed it down the hole. We saw the glimmer of water.

'It must be the Thames,' I said.

I know it sounds obvious, but in Leo's Lair it could have been anything. It could have been his own private shark pool.

'I'm going down,' my mum said. 'Just shine the light ahead of me so I can see where I'm putting my feet.'

We watched from the top as she climbed down. We lost sight of her before she reached the bottom but after a few minutes she came back up again.

'It's the Thames all right,' she said. 'You can see the lights on all the boats out there.'

'Can we swim to them?' Li said.

She shook her head. 'It's too far. It's far too cold and the current's too strong. It's like a millrace down there.'

'What about the boat you came in?' says Li.

'I was thinking about that,' she said, but she sounded doubtful. 'I left it under the tower with the searchlight, but it's not on any more and I don't know which one it is. You can't see much from down there.'

'It was next to the tower Leo blew up,' I said. I could remember watching from the window as she came towards us. She'd headed straight for the gap where the landing tower had been and then swung to the left.

'So you'd be able to see the gap from the water.'

'It would be about two hundred metres,' I said. 'I could easily do that.'

'I'm sure you could,' she said, 'in a proper swimming pool. But if you think I'm going to let you swim in the Thames Estuary at night in October you've got another thing coming.'

'But it's our only chance,' I said.

'I know.' She started to take her boots off.

'No!' I said. 'You can't. Not with your back.'

'Well, I'm not letting anyone else do it,' she said. 'Boys, do you mind giving us a little privacy?'

The two boys exchanged glances and then crawled back through the tunnel. I tried to reason with her.

'It's too far,' I said.

'Two hundred metres? I used to do that in less than two minutes – freestyle. One minute fifty-two was my best.'

'That was about thirty years ago,' I pointed out.

'Kit. It was fifteen at the most.'

'And before you broke your back.'

'Well, I'm not expecting to break any records this time,' she said. She was struggling out of her jeans. I started to plead with her then. I was nearly crying.

She took hold of my shoulders and looked into my eyes. 'I'll be all right,' she said. 'I know I'm a lot older, but I can still do two hundred metres, no problem.'

'But it's so cold.' I was shivering already with the trapdoor open, even up in Leo's playroom.

She was down to her bra and pants. 'If it's too cold,' she said, 'I'll come back. I never could stand the cold.'

Then she was gone.

I crouched at the side of the open trapdoor, peering down into the darkness. After a moment I remembered the car but all I could get out of the headlights was a feeble glow – the battery must have run down. I lay down full length at the edge of the hole but I couldn't see a thing and all I could hear was the sound of the waves sloshing about under the tower. I opened my mouth to shout down to her but then snapped it shut. The last thing I wanted to do was distract her while she was going down the ladder. I was convinced I'd never see her again. She was going to die and it would be my fault. If I hadn't lied to her, if I hadn't gone along with Nina's stupid ideas, if I'd never met Leo Lyall, she wouldn't be down there in that freezing darkness. We'd be out having a meal, all three of us, in a restaurant somewhere. The thought of that was almost too much to bear.

She must have reached the water now. I couldn't stand it any longer. I lowered myself through the hole, feeling for the rungs of the ladder with my feet. I counted them as I went down. When I reached twenty-two they started to feel all slimy and slippery and even colder than before. The next ones were dripping with seaweed. The smell of the sea was really strong down here – and the noise. It was like a large black animal rushing from side to side of its cage. Then, as I looked down, I could see it, the great black back of it rushing towards me and rearing up as it came, as if it was trying to snatch me down from the ladder into its jaws. There was no sign of my mother.

I clung on there, just above the highest surge, twisting round to look for her. I could just about make out the shapes of the two nearest towers and I could see the lights of the boats in the distance.

I could hear the sound of the helicopters, too, but they seemed a long way off.

It was so cold. My hands were freezing on the metal rungs of the ladder. I pushed my arm between two of the rungs, right up to my shoulder so I was wedged there. I clenched and unclenched my fingers to try and get some feeling in them. But if it was this cold for me, what must it be like for my mum? I couldn't believe she could possibly survive in that water. Not for more than a couple of minutes. And she must have been gone for at least ten.

I could feel my whole body starting to shiver. I was in danger of falling off the ladder and the sea seemed to be increasing its efforts to reach up and pull me down. There was a bit of feeling in my fingers, but not much. I knew that if I stayed down there much longer I wouldn't be able to climb back up the ladder. Part of me didn't care. If my mum was dead, I wanted to die too. But I was scared of dying in that water.

I heard the boat before I saw it. A different sound from the helicopters. More of a throbbing noise. Then I saw the white bow wave coming towards me and the black hull above it, like a moving patch of darkness. Then it was there, in among the legs of the tower, and I saw Mum at the tiller fighting to keep the boat steady in that surge of water. I was so relieved I nearly clapped my hands and fell off the ladder.

I was glad I'd come down now because she could throw a line to me. It was a different matter to catch it, though, with the state my hands were in. Then I had to tie it to the ladder. It took me ages and she was yelling at me in the end, telling me to get out of the way and let her do it. I really was sobbing now, but finally I managed it and she switched off the engine.

'G-g-g-go up the l-l-l-ladder,' she said. I could hardly understand her, her teeth were chattering so much. I climbed up a few rungs to make room for her but then I stopped and looked down to make sure she was all right. I could hardly cling on to the ladder myself and I was afraid she was going to fall off and I'd lose her, even at this stage. But she was pushing and prodding at me and yelling for me to 'k-k-k-keep g-g-g-going.' So I kept going.

I could see the square light that marked the open trapdoor high above me. It seemed as unreachable as the stars. I couldn't feel anything at all in my hands now. Any moment, I thought, I'm going to miss the next rung and fall back, taking Mum with me. She's right underneath me, shoving my bum from time to time. I suppose she meant to help.

We finally made it. I don't think I'd have got through the hole though, if Raoul and Li hadn't crawled back into the castle to help. They hauled us up and then Mum and I lay there, on the floor, shivering like a pair of stranded jellyfish. Mum was practically blue with cold. I'd heard the expression, but I never thought it could be literally true. Even her lips – there was no red in them at all. She looked like an alien.

Then I saw Raoul and Li looking at her with their eyes popping out. She was practically naked, of course. I made them take off their jackets and used them to dry her off, trying to rub some warmth into her. Then I helped her put her clothes back on.

'Get everyone together,' she said to the boys. 'Bring them in here.'

It didn't come out quite as easily as that but they understood. Or at least we thought they had. But after about five minutes they still hadn't come back.

'Go and see what they're doing,' Mum said.

When I crawled back through the gate I couldn't believe my eyes. The whole playroom was on the move. Cars, tanks, soldiers, planes, even the life-size

Dalek, trundling up and down, going, 'Exterminate, exterminate.' The din was incredible.

'What do you think you're doing?' I said.

'Li thinks the camera's sending a signal to the computer,' Raoul explained. 'And if there's no movement in the room, it sets off an alarm.'

I looked up at the camera on the wall. I suppose even Hal couldn't tell the difference between people moving and machines. But it still seemed crazy to me. Typical Li.

'OK,' I said, 'but I think you've got enough movement now. Get everyone in the castle.'

In fact, it wasn't possible to fit everyone in the castle at once. We had to start them off down the ladder while half of them were still waiting to crawl through the gate. It was going to take ages, and even if Hal was fooled it only needed Leo to check up on us and we'd be finished. If he saw us getting away he was mad enough to press the button and blow everything sky high.

Then Amor Gagalac said she wasn't going to crawl through the gate in case there were spiders.

You can imagine what Nina said to her.

Mum went down the ladder first so she could handle the boat. I followed, then Li, then Nina, then

the rest. Raoul was going to be last. I told him if
Lady Gagalac gave him any trouble he was to throw
her down. He looked at me like I was Lady Macbeth.

Somehow we managed to get them all down the
ladder, but getting them into the boat was a nightmare.
Mum went in first and started the outboard so she
could keep the boat more or less in position, but it
was rising and falling with every wave. You had to
wait until the boat was at its highest and then jump
off the ladder before it went down again. I managed
OK and so did Li and Nina. Then we just grabbed
the others and bundled them in one by one – until
we got to Amor. She was clinging on to the rungs
with both hands and sobbing. Me and Li were trying
to coax her but then Nina just shouts up to Raoul:
'Stamp on her fingers' and with a little scream Amor
let go and we grabbed her.

By the time Raoul got in we were so crowded we
couldn't move, and the boat was so low in the water
I thought we were going to be swamped any minute.

'Cast off!' Mum calls to me. Then, with the engine
on its lowest speed so we wouldn't make too many
waves, we moved out from under the tower.

We headed for the gap where the helipad had
been. I could see one of the broken legs sticking up

out of the sea. I thought if we can just get past it we'll be all right. But we were going so slowly – and even then the water was nearly breaking over the bow. The towers seemed to be leaning over us, giant insects glaring down at us as we headed for the gap. At any minute I thought some horrible iron claw was going to reach out and grab us. But finally we're through the gap and heading into the open estuary. I could hear the clatter of the helicopters much louder now and something else, a voice that sounded just like Leo's. Then I realized – it was 'Requiem for a Dying Planet'. It was blasting out from hidden speakers high in the towers.

Then suddenly we were bathed in light. At first I thought it was from the searchlight tower and Leo had spotted us at last. But it wasn't Leo; it was one of the helicopters. It was hovering directly above us. We were waving and shouting, as if they could hear us above all that noise.

Then lots of things happened at once.

First, something dropped from the helicopter and splashed into the water. It was so close I felt the spray on my face. Then this dark shape bobbed up in the water next to us. For one mad moment I thought it was a seal. But then I saw it was a man – a diver in a wetsuit. He was shouting something at us but it was impossible to hear him. Then there were two more of them, like black seals all around the boat.

Then there's another helicopter swooping out of the darkness, very low over the water. It had a searchlight on the front which pointed straight at one of the towers. And then I saw Leo Lyall. He was standing on the roof of the tower we'd just escaped from and he had something in his hands. It took me a moment to realize that it was a microphone and that he was either singing or miming into it. The whole thing, with the lights and the music and the towers and everything – it was like a setting for one of his rock concerts. Then there was a flash of even brighter light and something streaked out from the front of the helicopter leaving a trail of red fire behind it, like a rocket.

And then the tower goes up in a ball of flame.

Suddenly they were all going up – one after the other, exploding into flame as if it was some sort of chain reaction. A circle of flaming beacons. Everything lit up almost as bright as day. Red flames and black smoke rising up into the sky and the helicopter outlined against it, spinning round and round as if it was out of control. And the towers are like six giant bonfires with the flames leaping up to the stars. And there's a noise like a rolling clap of thunder, going on and on.

It was Leo Lyall's requiem and it was probably the most spectacular thing he'd ever done. And the last. There was no way he could have survived that. And you know what? I was sorry. He may have been crazy – he may have been going to blow us all up – but I'd never wanted him to die, not like that.

'Wow!' says Nina, getting it wrong again, because 'Wow' didn't even begin to do justice to what we were seeing.

'Apocalypse Now,' said Li, which was a bit more like it.

And then the wave hit us.

22

Emma

I'm standing on the stage at the Royal Albert Hall. The whole place is full of kids. Kids from all over the world. All under the age of thirteen, all delegates to the International Children's Conference on the Environment.

I'm standing there, holding the microphone and I have a sudden vision of Leo Lyall standing on the roof of the tower before the helicopter fired its missile and blew him and the rest of his fantasies into oblivion. Then I start to speak.

'The future,' I say, 'belongs to you.'

I look up and see them, all alone in the very back row of the balcony – 'the gods' I think they call it in the theatre, because it's so close to the ceiling – the

Spook and my grandmother. And it's as if they're there to remind me, as if I could ever forget: *The future belongs to you – but not to me.*

That's the dream and the nightmare.

It hasn't happened yet. The conference is still a dream and I'm not dead yet – otherwise I wouldn't be writing this.

We've got the money. The donations poured in from all over after what happened on the fort, and after Raoul's video went viral. The school governors said they don't mind any more – what else could they do with the whole world against them? We've even got new sponsors to replace Leo Lyall, and they don't seem to be totally insane. The conference will happen – and soon.

I just don't know if it will be soon enough for me.

I feel so tired all the time. The doctors say it's shock, a delayed reaction to what happened at the fort. They say it will soon wear off. But I don't know. I wonder if it's just the start of it.

But there is some hope – and I'll tell you why.

I told Raoul about the Spook. I felt I had to because we've become so close. I thought he'd laugh at me, but he didn't. He just gave me a big hug and said it was going to be all right. Then he told me the story of *A Christmas Carol* by Charles Dickens.

I knew it already, of course, but I let him tell me again because I like to hear the sound of his voice and the way he mixes up the words. It's much better than Dickens.

'There is this man, his name is Scrog.'

'No,' I said. 'Scrooge.'

He screwed his mouth up. 'Scooooooge.'

'That's right,' I said. 'Only not so many "o"s.'

'OK. Scoooge. He is a very bad man, very rich but very – what you say – *stringy*.'

'Stringy?' I was puzzled. I suppose Scrooge does look a bit stringy in the illustrations.

'Yes.' He frowned. 'I think. When you have the money but you do not wish to give to people.'

'Oh – *stingy*!' I said. 'Very stingy. Yes. Go on.'

'OK, well, on the eve of Noel he come home and there is a ghost on his door knicker.'

'Knocker,' I said, choking a sudden fit of the giggles.

'Nocker,' he said. 'What is nicker? Why you laugh?'

'Never mind,' I said. 'Go on.'

'OK, but not if you make the fun of me. It is not funny.'

'Sorry,' I said, trying to keep my face straight.

'OK. Well the ghost is of this man Marlon—'

'Marley,' I said.

'Marley.' But he's scowling now. 'Is better you do not speak again, OK?'

'OK,' I said.

'He is the friend of Scrooge—' He glares at me as if I'm going to say something. 'No, not friend. Scrooge has no friend. What is it he call him?'

'You want me to speak?'

He nodded.

'Partner. Business partner.'

'Business partner. Only he is dead. He die long time ago. But he is there on the door knicker— knocker. And later in Scrooge room. And he say to Scrooge – you very bad man, you end up in Hell like me . . .'

I was beginning to wonder where this story was going, because although I kind of knew it, it was a long time since I'd heard it – my dad used to read it to me at Christmas – and I'd forgotten most of the details. But what I could remember worried me a bit. I hoped Raoul didn't think I was like Scrooge. But wasn't this why he was telling me the story?

'And Marlon – Marley – he say to Scrooge, tonight

you get the visit by three ghost. The one is the Ghost of Christmas Past, the two is the Ghost of Christmas Present, and the three is the Ghost of Christmas Future. And during the night, this is what happen.

'The Ghost One, he show Scrooge what he is like in Christmas past – long time ago when he is little boy. Very happy, very kind and everyone love him. The Ghost Two is what he is now – very bad, very *stingy*. And all the world hate him. The Ghost Three he show the future. The Christmas next year. And Scrooge is dead. And no one is sorry. And he show Scrooge—' He frowned again. 'What you say for this, the hole with the stone?'

'I can speak?'

He nodded again.

'A grave.'

'He show Scrooge a grave. With Scrooge name – Ebenezer Scrooge. And Scrooge he go like this.' He knelt down on his knees and put his hands together as if he was praying. '"Please Mr Ghost of Christmas Future" – he is big fat man this ghost, like Father Christmas – "please Mr Ghost, say is not true. Say I not die. Not yet." And he say he get better, he change, he be very good, like before. And the ghost finger it start to w-w-w— what you say when it do this?' He waggled his finger about.

'Waver,' I said. 'But what are you trying to say? That if I change . . .'

'If you change,' he finished for me, 'you do not die. Yes. Like Scrooge.'

'So you want me to change?' I said. 'You don't like me the way I am?'

'No. No.' He looked horrified, as if he'd suddenly realized that it might seem like that. He was still on his knees and he could stay there so far as I was concerned, if that's what he meant. 'No. I do not mean that I do not like you now. I like you very much. No, but you change from what it is you – you – you—'

'What I might become?' I finished for him.

'Yes,' he said with relief. He was beginning to sweat. 'You change from what you might become. Which is good,' he said. 'Because I do not want you to become an emu.'

The other thing that happened was to do with my dad.

He and my mum were getting on much better. In fact, the difference was amazing. Mum seemed to have changed completely since her adventures on

Fort Doom. She'd even become famous again for a while – though she didn't seem to be too impressed by that. But there was talk of her getting a job as a sports commentator on television, because of her swimming background. Which was fantastic, but the really amazing thing was that she'd stopped cleaning the house all the time. My dad was spending far more time at home and my mum was being much nicer to him and it was a much happier place to be.

It's a tip, of course – the whole place is like my room – but I can live with that. It's just great to have my dad home all the time – and happy. He says it was the fear of losing us.

'It was the thing I was always afraid of, you know? All those terrible things I see when I'm working. War and violence and what it does to people. Children especially. I think I was scared I'd bring it back home with me. And the next thing I knew it'd be happening to you and your mum. It was like it haunted me.'

We were walking across the Common together on our way back from one of my football matches. (We won 3–2 and I scored one of the goals.) And suddenly he starts off, like it's been building up for years and he's got to let it out.

'I couldn't bear the thought of it. I thought, if

I don't *care*, then it won't happen; I won't get hurt. Like the kind of barrier you put up when you're covering something horrible, like a war. Looking through a lens. Like life through a viewfinder. You have to do that, to some extent – it's a way of protecting yourself. But when you were both out on that fort . . .' He shook his head. 'There was nothing, no barrier high enough or wide enough to stop me from . . . to stop me *feeling*.'

I wondered if he knew Mum had told him that I knew about her and Leo Lyall. I think she probably had, but he never mentioned it.

What he did mention, though, was much more important in the end. To me, anyway.

'Your mum had a very rough time, you know,' he said suddenly, after we'd been walking along saying nothing for a bit, 'with what happened to her own mother.'

I looked at him in surprise. He'd said it as if I knew all about it. But I hadn't said anything to him – not about the newspaper cutting I'd found or anything.

'What do you mean?' I said.

'Well, the fire and everything, you know?' He looked at me, frowning slightly. 'Remember? I told you.'

'No,' I shook my head. 'Told me what?'

'You know – how she'd left the gas on and there was this explosion?'

I didn't say anything but I nodded as if I was thinking about it, so he'd go on.

'Well, you can imagine what your mum felt about it. You know, all that grief – and guilt.'

'Guilt?' I said. 'What had she got to feel guilty about? It wasn't her fault.'

'No, but that's what she felt. She felt as if she was responsible. You know, for not going to see her so much, being put off by the drinking. I probably didn't tell you that. Your nan really hit the bottle at the end, and who can blame her, eh, with being so ill? But it didn't make it any easier for your mum. And of course she felt terrible about the girl.'

'The girl?' I said. 'What girl?'

'The girl they found in the garden. A few days later. Under all the debris. And then they found all this stuff in the shed – the garden shed. I think your mum felt, you know, if she'd gone around there more, she'd have probably realized.'

'Realized what?' I had no idea what he was on about.

'That she'd been sleeping there. In the shed.'

'Who'd been sleeping where?' I said. 'What shed?'

'I'm sure I told you about the girl,' he frowned. 'Didn't I?' He looked puzzled as if he was wondering whether he had or not. I almost screamed at him.

'*What girl?*'

'The girl they found in the garden. Under the ruins. The other body.'

I felt a shiver run up my spine. I didn't know it could really happen, that. But I really did feel the hairs prickling on the back of my neck.

'They think she'd been sleeping there – in the shed. Your nan probably didn't even know about it.'

'What do you mean?' I said again. 'Who was she?'

'Well, they never found out. Probably some poor, homeless kid. She had a chain round her neck with a name on it – Emma. But no one knows if it was her name or someone else's. She might have found it somewhere, or stolen it. The body was never identified.'

'How old was she?' I said. My voice sounded very distant, as if it belonged to someone else.

'About fourteen or fifteen. They didn't know for sure.'

'And she was killed by the fire?'

'More by the blast, I think.' Then he looked at me

sharply. 'I'm sure I told you about all of this.'

'When?' I practically shouted at him. 'When did you tell me about it?'

'Oh, I don't know, a year or two ago. You asked me something about your nan. I thought you should know. You really can't remember?'

'No. And you told me about this girl – Emma?'

'Yeah. At least I think I did.' He nodded to himself. 'Yeah, I'm sure I did.'

There was no reason for him to lie about it. I can't have been listening. Or else I'd blanked it out. I'd read about people doing that. Blanking out something that they didn't want to hear, or that was too awful for them to think about. But it stays there, in a dark part of your mind where all the secrets are buried.

'What happened to her?' I said.

'The girl? I told you . . .'

'No – what happened to her body?'

'Well, it was buried.' He looked surprised that I should ask. 'We went to the funeral. In fact, we paid for it. The funeral, the grave, everything. Even flowers. Your mum was really insistent about it.'

'So where is she buried?'

'In West Norwood. One of the old Victorian graveyards they built all around London. It's very beautiful. I mean, for a graveyard. Very, you know, *Gothic*. Why do you want to know?'

I went there with Raoul. It was a Saturday morning and we went on our bikes. It's famous, West Norwood cemetery. I checked it out on Google. There are lots of famous people buried there. But it's not just because of that, it's because it's – well, the only word for it is spooky. I know all graveyards are supposed to be spooky but some are more spooky than others, and this is spooky in a beautiful kind of way. I suppose that's what Dad means by Gothic.

You have to go there to understand. There are all these wonderful tombs, like something out of *Dracula*. And it's surrounded by very high walls and railings, because when it was built there were people called body snatchers who dug up the bodies just after they were buried and sold them to medical students to practise on. Whole areas are overgrown, like a wilderness or a wood, and the graves are covered with ivy and brambles which makes them all that much more interesting, at least to me. But other parts have been cleared and tidied up by volunteers. They've stopped burying people there now – I think Emma must have been one of the last – or else they got special permission for her.

She was buried in the children's section. This is the saddest part. All these tiny graves with their headstones and inscriptions. There was one that just said: *We loved you so much but we miss you more*. It almost broke my heart; I couldn't read any more. And there were all these stone angels, like ghosts among the trees. It was early November and there was a faint mist in the air and frost on the ground. It was so cold we were wrapped up in hats and scarves and gloves and our breath froze in the air. That was like ghosts, too.

She was at the end of one of the paths, where the trees began. A simple white headstone. No inscription. Just the one word – 'Emma' – and the date: 1986–2001.

I took the flowers out of my bag. A small bunch of violets. I'd brought a jam jar to put them in. I took my gloves off and arranged them neatly by the headstone, as neat as I'll ever be able to manage, anyway. Then I stood back and looked at it. It wasn't much. Just a small, sad bunch of flowers, a dark splash of violet against the frost.

'Thank you,' I said.

'Is OK,' Raoul said. He was pouring water from

one of the watering cans that were lying around. 'Is no problem. There is no football today. The ground is too hard.'

'Idiot,' I said. 'Not you. *Her*. She saved my life. Twice. Once when I fell under the bus and once in the fort.' Then I asked the question that had been bothering me for some time. 'Why do you think she did that?'

He shrugged. 'Maybe she want you to come and put the flowers on her grave,' he said. 'She want somebody to remember her.'

It was a nice thought, even if he doesn't believe it. He doesn't really believe in ghosts; he thinks it's all in the mind. And maybe it is.

'But why me?'

'Maybe because you are so nice?' He grinned, but he could see I wasn't convinced.

'But she seemed to hate me,' I said.

'Well – maybe it is your grandmama. Maybe she was nice to her. Maybe she help her or something. So she has to help you.'

I stared at him. 'What did you say?'

He started to say it again.

Then I realized. 'Oh my god,' I said. 'It was her!'

'Where?' He looked around him in alarm as if I'd

just seen her lurking in the background. He might say he doesn't believe in ghosts, but he's not taking any chances.

'The fire,' I said. 'It wasn't my nan, it was *her*! She got in the house and she turned on the gas.'

He was looking at me the way Nina does sometimes, as if I've totally lost it.

'She was trying to kill herself – but she killed my nan as well. And now it's like she has to make up for it. And she can't rest in peace until she has.'

I was sure I was right. I couldn't wait to get home and tell Mum, so she could stop feeling guilty.

'OK,' Raoul said. He was nodding as if this made sense to him. 'Well, maybe now she will rest,' he said, 'and leave you alone.'

He took my hand and we walked back to where we'd left our bikes. As we reached them I had a sudden memory of the first time I'd seen her, when I was trapped under the bike and the bus was coming at me. It could have been me lying there in a grave and my mum and dad bringing flowers for me.

I felt the tears coming then and I brushed them away angrily with the back of my hand. And Raoul put his arm around me and said I shouldn't be so sad.

'You will not be like her,' he says. He thinks I'm

still worried about that. 'Nobody loves her. That is why she is the way she is. But everybody loves you.'

Sometimes he manages to say exactly the right thing, but it didn't make me feel any less sad, because I was feeling sad for her, not me.

Just before we rode off I thought I saw her watching us from among the trees. But it was probably a statue.

SPOOKED –
Fact and Fiction

Although this is a work of fiction I have used some true facts and real places in the story.

The World War Two forts in the Thames are real and you can still see them – much as I've described – if you take a boat ride into the Thames Estuary. They're called the Maunsell Forts after the man who designed them and they were towed out into the Thames in 1943 and armed with anti-aircraft guns to deter German planes from flying up the river to bomb London. They shot down a good few of them along with a number of unmanned flying bombs, but after the war there was no more use for them and they were abandoned.

No more use as forts, perhaps. But some people saw other functions for them. Several of them became pirate radio stations. One of them was run by a rock singer called Screaming Lord Sutch. Another fort has been declared an independent state. The Principality of Sealand. It has its own currency and sells peerages, much the same as England. There is no Fort Doom – I made that up – but there is a fort called the Shivering Sands.

The Wailing Monk of Bec also existed in real life. It was the nickname of an eleventh-century monk called Gundulf, from the abbey of Bec in Normandy. He was a great architect and built the Tower of London for William the Conqueror. The land now known as Tooting Bec was given by King William to the monks of the abbey but as far as I know it's not haunted, either by the Wailing Monk or anyone else.

However, when I began writing this I thought the most difficult thing to believe was not the story of the ghosts, but the idea of an eleven-year-old setting out to organize an international children's conference on the environment. But this is something that really happened and involved my own son, Dermot. The conference was called 'Leave It To Us' and brought in 800 children's delegates from 90 countries around the world. The day it ended, Dermot flew to New York by Concorde to present their demands – and plan of action – to the UN.

Over the next year or so Dermot was invited to address adult environmental conferences in Canada, South Korea and Brazil. In 1998 the United Nations Environment Programme elected the Junior Board to the prestigious ranks of its Youth Environment Global Roll of Honour for their outstanding contributions to the protection of the environment. Dermot now runs the charity English for Action, which provides free, community-based lessons in English to people who speak other languages, and supports them in action to help improve their lives and communities. The character of Kit, however, is entirely fictitious and I think Dermot would like it to be known that he has never seen a ghost or tweeted about a lost hamster.

Paul Bryers
www.paulbryers.com

Acknowledgements

A special thanks to Emma Donald, Shannon Harris and Laura Hasson who were studying one of my books for their creative writing course at Winchester University and very generously shared their own experiences of the transition from childhood to adolescence. Also: Theo Christie and his father John, Eloise and Eva Lamb, my own daughter Elesa, and Annie Feinburgh who read the first draft and suggested a number of improvements; the children and teachers of several schools in South London who set up focus groups for me to discuss some of the issues involved in the novel – I won't name them in case anyone jumps to the wrong conclusion that the fictitious school in the novel is based on one of them; Hira Saeed who helped me with some specific information on Muslim girls; Leslie Hampson who shared his surprising insights on goths and emos; Michael and Kitty Ann, who initiated the first international children's conference on the environment at Eastbourne; my son Dermot who was one of the two junior hosts at the conference; and of course, Beverley Birch, who commissioned the novel for Hodder and helped me with her expertise, not only as an editor, but as a writer and the mother of two daughters.